She looked up into the jet gleam of his eyes and felt the automatic quickening of her heart. *Don't react,* she told herself fiercely. *Don't let him see that you're acutely aware of him as a man, rather than a boss.*

"G-good morning, Jack."

"Good morning, Ashley."

Curving her lips into a pleasant smile, she tilted her head in question, wishing that he would move away a little—at least, far enough for her not to have to inhale his delicious raw scent. "Can I do something for you, Jack?"

For a moment Jack silently cursed her innocent question. *Could she do something for him?* She most certainly could. Thoughts began with a sudden and inexplicable kiss and ended with seeing that calm smile of hers dissolving into out-of-control pleasure. Erotic and distracting thoughts he should *not* have been having about his secretary. Not in any circumstances, but especially not in his own particular circumstances…

The Powerful and the Pure

When Beauty tames the brooding beast...

From Mr. Darcy to Heathcliff,
the best romantic heroes have always been tall,
dark and *dangerously* irresistible.

This year, indulge yourself as Harlequin Presents®
brings you four formidable men—the ultimate
heroes. Untamable...or so they think!

Watch out for these four timeless love stories in
Harlequin Presents!

Available wherever Harlequin books are sold or
online at eHarlequin.com.

Sharon Kendrick

THE FORBIDDEN WIFE

TORONTO NEW YORK LONDON
AMSTERDAM PARIS SYDNEY HAMBURG
STOCKHOLM ATHENS TOKYO MILAN MADRID
PRAGUE WARSAW BUDAPEST AUCKLAND

Recycling programs
for this product may
not exist in your area.

ISBN-13: 978-0-373-12995-9

THE FORBIDDEN WIFE
Previously published in the U.K. as THE FORBIDDEN INNOCENT

First North American Publication 2011

Copyright © 2011 by Sharon Kendrick

THE FORBIDDEN WIFE

This book is dedicated to
Anna Wilson—a brilliant wife, mother,
daughter, doctor and friend.
Love lives on.

CHAPTER ONE

THE last thing she wanted was a walk. The air was raw and the grey skies heavy but Ashley was jittery. Her morning had been spent on a stuffy train, watching the bleak and unfamiliar landscape whizzing by while she psyched herself up to meet her new boss. Telling herself that there was no *need* to be jittery and that he couldn't possibly be as intimidating as the woman at the employment agency had implied.

Unfortunately, her arrival at his imposing manor house had done little to reassure her—because the powerful and wealthy Jack Marchant wasn't there. And when she'd asked Christine—his part-time housekeeper—when he was expected, the middle-aged woman had raised her eyes to heaven in that *you-tell-me* kind of way.

'Oh, you never can tell with Mr Marchant,' she'd pronounced airily. 'That man is a law unto himself.'

Now, as Ashley made her way along the frozen lane, flexing her fingers inside her woollen gloves to try to keep them warm, she realised that Jack Marchant seemed to have a daunting effect on women of a certain age. The woman at the employment agency had already described him as 'formidable'—a word which covered a multitude of sins, in Ashley's experience. Did that mean he was bad-tempered and bossy—or just rude enough not to bother turning up to meet his new secretary?

Not that it mattered what he was like—his personality was irrelevant. Ashley needed this job and she needed the money. Badly. It was a lucrative short-term contract and she could put up with pretty much anything—even this brooding northern landscape where the air seemed so cold and so biting.

She still wasn't good at change—even with all the practice she'd had growing up in the care system, and then being passed from one foster family to another. She still got that claustrophobic feeling of dread whenever she had to meet new people and ease herself into a different situation. Learning what people liked—and, more importantly, what they didn't like. Listening out for what they said—but looking in their eyes to see what they really *meant*.

Because almost from the cradle, she had learnt to read between the lines. To differentiate between words and intent. To trace the truth behind a smile. She had learned her lessons well. It had been a survival technique at which she had grown to excel and one she still instinctively practised all the time.

Her fingers fractionally warmer now, she stood still for a moment as she looked around her. Leafless trees stood sentry over the bare branches of the high hedgerows and over to the left lay the wild expanse of the moors. It was a lonely place, she thought—with a stark and austere air to it. But as she walked further up the incline of the lane towards the brow of a hill she could see the distant spire of a church and the jumble of rooftops. So at least there was a village—with people and shops and who knew what else?

And if she turned to look the other way, she could see Blackwood Manor spread out below her. From this distance, it looked even more imposing than when she'd been inside—its elegant grey form straddling the land and making her realise just how large the house was. From here she could see its dark woods and the scattering of outbuildings—as well as the distant glitter of a lake.

She looked down at the estate and tried to imagine what it must be like to own that much land. Was that what made Jack Marchant so 'formidable'? Did having buckets of money corrupt you, as people often said it did? She was so lost in this particular daydream that at first she barely registered an unexpected sound until it grew louder, and closer. An unfamiliar noise was reverberating through the air and it took a few seconds for Ashley to realise that a horse was approaching.

Taken off guard, she felt disorientated—a feeling which only increased when she saw a colossal black shape thundering down the lane towards her. It was a huge beast of a thing, which looked as if it had sprung straight from some childhood nightmare—its powerful limbs rippling beneath the dark silk of its glossy coat.

On its back was a man who, stupidly, wasn't wearing a protective helmet, so that the wind streamed through his raven hair. Ashley blinked.

She became aware of faded blue jeans, a powerful body—and a face which was hard and forbidding. And she found herself staring into a pair of steely eyes—eyes as black and fathomless as a starless night.

Standing transfixed in the middle of the lane, she was stilled as much by the expression on the man's face as the sensation of seeing such an enormous animal at such close quarters. But suddenly the horse seemed almost on top of her and she jumped out of the way with a little yelp. Instantly, the horse reared up in alarm—just as a large black and white dog rushed out from one of the hedgerows and began to chase after it.

Suddenly, everything became a blur and she heard a succession of noises. Another whinnying sound. A muffled but furious curse—followed by a sickening thud—before the horse crumpled to the ground, swiftly followed by the man riding it.

The dog was barking dementedly. It came running up to her—as if demanding that she help—and Ashley rushed forward, scared at what she might find. The horse struggled to its feet, but the prone shape of the rider was terrifyingly still. Fear clutched at her throat as she crouched down beside him and bent over him. Was he…was he…*dead*? Her heart raced as she touched his shoulder with shaking fingers. 'Hello? Hello? Are you okay?'

The man moaned and Ashley winced. 'Can you

hear me?' she questioned urgently—because hadn't she read somewhere that you were supposed to keep injured people from drifting into unconsciousness? 'I said—*can you hear me*?'

'Of course I can hear you—when you're inches away from my ear and bellowing into it!'

His voice was deep and surprisingly strong—and more than a little irritated. Thick lashes parted by a fraction to reveal a gleam of the steely eyes she'd seen just before he'd fallen and Ashley felt a huge rush of relief flood over her. He was alive!

'Are you hurt?' she questioned.

He grimaced as he stared up into a wide pair of anxious eyes and trembling lips and his own mouth hardened. What a stupid question! Why act concerned when it was her own stupid behaviour which had caused the fall in the first place? 'What do you think?' he questioned sardonically as, gingerly, he moved his leg.

For a moment Ashley was distracted by the movement and even more by the muscular thigh which was covered in faded denim. She swallowed. 'Can I…can I do anything?'

'Well, you could start by giving me some space,' he growled. 'Stand back, woman—and let me breathe.'

His voice was so authoritative that Ashley found herself obeying him, watching as he tried to stand up—but he didn't make it any further than kneeling. At this, the dog went completely crazy—barking and leaping at the man until he silenced it with a terse command.

'Quiet, Casey!'

He seemed to slump—before sitting back down heavily in the lane and, instinctively, Ashley moved closer. 'Look, you really shouldn't move.'

'How do you know what I should do?'

'I read it in a first-aid book. And if you're hurt—which clearly you are—then I could go and get help. I think you should stay put. I've got my mobile, I can ring for an ambulance. You might have broken something.'

Impatiently, he shook his dark head. 'I haven't broken anything. It's probably just a strain—and certainly nothing to fuss about. Wait a minute.' At this, he tried standing again, and then groaned.

Ashley didn't move as he gathered his breath, taking the opportunity to have a closer look at him. Because he was the kind of man who made you want to keep on looking...

Even his current crumpled stance couldn't hide his impressive height, the broad sweep of his shoulders or the powerful, denim-clad legs. His windswept hair was raven-black and his eyes looked blacker still. At some time he might have been in a fight—or perhaps an accident—for there was a tiny scar by the side of his lips. Sensual lips, Ashley found herself thinking—though their cushioned curves were outlined by a hardness which seemed to have been stamped on them indelibly. Perhaps because they were twisted in pain from his fall.

His features were too rugged to be described as conventionally handsome—but something about his presence made him seem compelling. He exuded a rampant masculinity which should have unnerved her—but oddly enough, did not. Because in that moment—wasn't he injured, and therefore a little vulnerable?

'I can't possibly think of leaving you—not like this,' she said stubbornly.

He shook his head. 'Of course you can! It's getting late and these lanes aren't good to walk on in the dark. Especially when the cars come speeding along.' Granite-hard eyes bored into her curiously. 'Or maybe you know the area well?'

'No,' she said. 'Not at all well.'

'No, I guess if you did you'd have realised you shouldn't stand motionless in a blind spot in the path of a galloping horse,' he said drily, his hand rubbing at the back of his neck as he flicked her another look. 'Where do you live?'

'Actually, I've just moved to the area today.'

'Oh?'

It seemed foolish in the light of his accident and the fact that she was crouching rather uncomfortably in a damp lane to be discussing what *she* was doing there. But there was something so insistent about the way he was looking at her—those hard black eyes firing out a question—which made it impossible for her not to answer. And impossible for her not to feel a little dizzy… as if he were sucking all the strength from her with that strange, searing gaze of his. 'To Blackwood Manor,' she said.

Black brows arrowed together and his lips quirked

into an odd kind of smile. 'Ah. So you live *there*, do you—the grey house which overlooks the moorland?'

Ashley nodded. Strange to think that the imposing manor was now her home. 'Yes.' She gave a little wriggle of her shoulders. 'It's not mine, of course. The house belongs to my new boss.'

'Really?' he mused, his black eyes flicking over her. 'And what's he like, this new boss of yours?'

'I don't know. I haven't met him yet—he was out when I arrived. I'm his new PA—well, I'm more of a secretary really. He's…' She was about to start telling him that she'd been employed to type his novel for him but suddenly Ashley halted, feeling a fool—and wondering why on earth she was telling this complete stranger her business. Was it something to do with that intense way he had of looking at her? Or the fact that it seemed easier to talk than to focus on the odd prickling of her senses, which seemed to stem from his rather daunting proximity.

She began to scramble to her feet to put some distance between them. Discretion was a necessary part of being someone's personal assistant—and what if Mr Marchant got wind of the fact that she'd been blabbing indiscriminately to someone she'd just met? 'Actually, I'd better get going, if you're absolutely sure there's nothing I can do,' she said hurriedly. 'He might be back by now and I wouldn't want to keep him waiting.'

'Hold on a moment,' he said suddenly as he prepared to stand up. 'You can help me if you want. Just catch hold of my horse, will you?'

It was the first time that Ashley had even considered the riderless horse and now she glanced over at it. A great big powerhouse of a beast—it was even more intimidating than its rider. Standing a little way down the lane, it was stamping its hooves in turn and snorting great clouds of smoky breath into the chilly atmosphere.

'Or are you afraid?' he questioned silkily, his gaze running over her face and lingering there.

She felt more fearful of that brilliant black gaze than of anything the horse could throw at her—but Ashley knew enough about self-preservation to realise when it was necessary to admit ignorance.

'I don't really know anything about horses,' she confessed.

He nodded. 'Then don't go near him. I'll manage,' he said. 'Hold still.'

Placing his hand on Ashley's shoulder, he rose slowly to his feet and she experienced the weirdest sensation as his fingers pressed into her flesh. Was it because she had so rarely been touched by a man that it felt suddenly *intimate*? As if that brief touch had scorched through her clothes to the chilled body beneath—setting her skin on fire. Little flames of something unfamiliar licked at the pit of her stomach and she swallowed as he steadied himself.

In the cool of the darkening afternoon, their eyes met and Ashley felt as if she were melting beneath the scorching impact of his gaze. Was it her imagination or did his mouth tighten and a little nerve begin to flicker at his temple? Was she alone in the bizarre thought that somehow it felt as if the most natural thing in the world was for him to take her in his arms? And to then crush her against that hard, powerful body of his... She felt her mouth dry and then, abruptly, he pulled away and began to walk slowly towards his horse, making small crooning noises beneath his breath as he approached it.

Mesmerised, Ashley watched him as he sprang onto his horse—the way she'd seen it done countless times on TV. And it was as if his fall and the fact that he'd been temporarily winded had been nothing but a figment of her imagination—for he made the movement look completely effortless. It was poetry in motion, she thought as he leaned over and patted the animal's flank and then glanced up to find her eyes still fixed on him.

For one insane moment she wanted to beg him not to go—to stay and make her feel properly alive again—so that she could experience that strange and disconcerting clamour of her senses once more. But the insanity passed as she looked up at him.

'Thanks for your help,' he said abruptly. 'Now go. Quickly. Before it gets dark and you startle some other hapless person with those big, wide eyes of yours. Casey! Here, boy!' The dog came running up and the man tightened his knees around the horse's sides—sending Ashley one final mocking look before he began to canter off down the lane.

For a moment, Ashley didn't move—she just stood watching as they faded into the distance, the lengthening shadows of the lane gradually swallowing them up as the clopping sound of hooves died away. Her fingers moved to her face to rest beneath her eyes. Nobody had ever told her they were big and wide before—and certainly not anybody who looked like *that*. Just who *was* the rugged stranger with the powerful body and the brooding expression? she wondered.

Her walk now abandoned, she made her way back towards Blackwood Manor—and when a tight-lipped Christine opened the door, a large black and white dog shot forward and began jumping up.

'Casey!' said Ashley without thinking as the animal instantly began licking at her hand. But Christine seemed too preoccupied to notice that she knew the dog's name—and Ashley's thoughts buzzed in confusion as she wondered what it was doing here. Swallowing down a mixture of panic and excitement, she turned to the housekeeper. 'Whose dog is that?'

'It belongs to Mr Marchant.'

'Is he…is he back then?'

Christine nodded. 'Oh, he came back all right, but not for long.' Her face was grim. 'Actually, he's had an accident.'

'An accident?' said Ashley as the knot in the pit of her stomach began to tighten.

'Yes, tumbled off his horse just down the lane from here. He's driven himself off to the hospital for an X-ray.'

The dog. An accident. The sudden recognition of what the word 'formidable' really meant. Little pieces of reality began to lock together to form a bigger picture which suddenly became crystal-clear.

And Ashley's heart began to pound as she realised just who the man on the horse had been. Her brand-new boss—Jack Marchant.

CHAPTER TWO

THE bare branches of the tree rattled wildly against Ashley's window but she barely heard them as she stared out into the garden. All she could think about was the man with the hard black eyes who had fallen from his horse—and how she had unwittingly tumbled across her new boss in the most bizarre of circumstances.

Her new boss.

She swallowed down her panic. Was he hurt? *Badly* hurt? Lying even now in some sterile cubicle at the local accident and emergency department—with some slow haemorrhage seeping all the lifeblood out of him? So that maybe she would never get the chance to see him or speak to him again.

She wondered what the X-ray would show—because she knew how life could change in a heartbeat. One moment, you could be out galloping and enjoying life and the next… She swallowed. What if he had been badly injured—and if that were the case, then hadn't she been a fool for letting him ride off alone like that?

But Christine had said there was no news—and

nothing for her to do until Mr Marchant returned—
and so Ashley had gone to her own room, to quieten her
thudding heart and try to calm herself. And once she
had washed her hands and brushed her hair she looked
around at the subdued comfort of her brand-new room
to try to calm her ruffled nerves.

She was more used to accommodation the size of a
shoe-box but this one was huge. There was a queen-sized
bed covered with a cashmere throw—as well as extra
blankets in the cupboard, since Christine had warned
her that these northern temperatures could plummet.
A sofa heaped with cushions overlooked the gardens
and there was a small television set perched on top of a
beautiful chest of drawers.

'Mr Marchant doesn't really watch a lot of television
and we don't have it on much downstairs,' Christine had
confided. 'But I told him that you can't bring people
out into the middle of nowhere without giving them
anything to entertain themselves of an evening!'

Ashley had smiled. No, she couldn't really imagine
the brooding Jack Marchant huddled over a soap opera
or some kind of reality game show.

Actually, she wasn't a great fan of TV herself and,
pulling a paperback from the small pile of books she'd
brought with her, she sat down and began to read as
she waited for news from the hospital. But for once the
words failed to conjure up the power to take her into the
imaginary world she preferred to the real-life version.
Instead, she kept seeing images of that powerful body
lying crumpled and temporarily winded.

So *that* had been Jack Marchant. She had been expecting someone older—and more remote. Some bespectacled and crusty academic, perhaps—as befitted the author of several well-received military biographies who was branching out into novel-writing. But he had been the very opposite of that. Different, in fact, from anyone she'd ever met.

Her book forgotten, she hugged her arms around her chest. Ashley had mixed with plenty of boys when she'd been growing up, but they had been just that—boys— with all their swagger and bravado. Whereas the man who had leaned on her today had exuded a commanding masculinity she'd never experienced before. And she wasn't quite sure how she was going to deal with someone like that on a day-to-day basis.

But you don't have to deal with anything other than the work he gives you to do, taunted a small voice inside her head. *He's your boss, remember? You type his work for him, you live quietly in his house—and at the end of every month you collect the generous salary he's providing. That's the reason you're here, after all.*

Her thoughts were broken by a sudden tap on her bedroom door—and she opened it to find Christine standing there, with her coat on and a battered shopping bag looped over her arm.

'I'm just off home now,' she said. 'And Mr Marchant's back from the hospital. He's downstairs in the library and said he'd like to meet you.'

'Is he okay?' Ashley asked quickly.

'Oh, he's fine. It'd take a lot more than a tumble from his horse to damage someone like *him*.'

But Ashley felt a fluttery kind of nervousness at the thought of seeing him again and, self-consciously, her hands skimmed down over her sweater and alighted on the waistband of her jeans.

'Maybe I'd better change,' she said doubtfully.

'Maybe you had,' said Christine. 'But better not keep him waiting too long—he doesn't like to be kept waiting. I'll see you in a couple of days. Have fun.'

Fun? Now why did Ashley get the distinct feeling that there wasn't going to be much fun involved in this new position?

After Christine had gone, she put on a plain skirt and a neat blouse, brushed and twisted her long hair into a French plait and then went downstairs to the library. The door was closed and the deeply growled and peremptory command of 'Come!' in response to her hesitant tapping almost made her lose her nerve and turn away.

Pushing open the heavy door, she saw a dark figure standing by the fire with his back to her—a figure she recognised instantly and yet one that seemed even more intimidating than it had done earlier. Was that because the red flames threw his tall figure into a stark silhouette which seemed to dominate the room? Or because his physique was, quite simply, breathtaking?

Suddenly, she felt insubstantial in the presence of such a remarkable package of masculinity. As if he could dominate her as he dominated the room… It was another unwanted moment of awareness and Ashley found herself struggling to make his name pass her dry lips.

'Mr…Marchant?'

He turned then and the flames illuminated his face—sending shifting shadows across features which were so still that they might have been fashioned from dark marble. He seemed to have a sense of total isolation about him—as if he had cut himself off from the rest of the world—and as Ashley stared at him she saw the brief flicker of something bleak in his eyes. Something like pain. And something like anger. And then it was gone. Instead, his look became coolly assessing as his gaze swept over her, though it was a moment before he spoke.

'So, we meet again.'

'Yes.'

That same odd smile she'd seen earlier once again curved his sensual lips. 'My lady rescuer.'

Ashley shrugged her shoulders awkwardly. 'I didn't really do very much to rescue you.'

'No. I suppose you didn't.' Jack studied her, remembering her wide eyes and trembling lips. The softness of her touch as she had shaken him… How potent gentleness could be, he thought suddenly. And how long since he had felt its subtle seduction? He flicked the thought away—even though his attention was momentarily distracted by the faint swell of her breasts beneath her sweater. 'And no doubt you were too stricken by guilt to be of much use in any case,' he challenged huskily.

'*Guilt?*' she echoed defensively, as unwittingly

he touched a raw nerve. Because hadn't her life been blighted by false accusations made by those on whom she depended? The foster mothers. The matrons in the care homes. Time after time she had discovered that the disadvantaged were an easy target. And now, as she looked into his hard black eyes, she wondered if here was someone else who would concoct crimes she was supposed to have committed. 'I wasn't aware that I'd done something wrong.'

'Don't you know that it's inadvisable to startle horses? That they're as temperamental as women?' he said. 'But don't stand over there by the door looking so nervous. You'd better come in and sit down—I won't bite! And if we're to spend the next few months incarcerated together, then I'd better know something about you—don't you think? Sit down—no, not there. Sit over here by the lamp, where I can see you properly.'

She was acutely aware of his piercing gaze and authoritative manner, and Ashley's legs felt curiously jelly-like as she walked to the spot he'd indicated. Perching herself on the edge of the chair, she watched as he lowered himself into a similar one on the opposite side of the fireplace—though his own seat was more shadowed, she realised. Which meant that she couldn't see him so well as he had insisted on seeing her...

He had changed from the faded jeans into dark trousers and an expensive-looking shirt of silk, which hinted at the hard body beneath. With the more formal clothes, he now looked every inch the modern-day aristocrat—

his long legs stretched out in front of him as he surveyed her from between narrowed and watchful eyes.

'You're much younger than I thought,' he observed, his eyes drifting over the smooth surface of her skin, and he felt a flicker of irritation. Why the hell had the agency sent him someone like this—someone with that tight bloom of youth on her skin, which women spent the rest of their lives hopelessly trying to recapture?

Ashley gave a little shrug. 'The agency didn't specify an age, Mr Marchant.'

'No, please don't call me that.' He shook his head and gave a dismissive little wave of his hand. 'I don't like any kind of formality. Not now that I've left the army. You'd better call me Jack.'

Jack. It suited him. A strong and powerful name. The name of a man who wouldn't suffer fools gladly. Jack. She tried it again silently in her head until his deep voice broke into her reverie.

'And you're Ashley?' he questioned impatiently, wondering if she was going to adopt that dreamy expression every time he spoke to her.

'That's right. Ashley Jones.'

'And how old are you, Ashley Jones?'

'Eighteen.'

'Eighteen?' He made a small sound of annoyance underneath his breath. She was even younger than he'd thought. He studied her, acknowledging once again that there was something distracting about dewy-eyed youth—something which drifted temptation in front of a man, even if he had no intention of being tempted.

It made him think about sex—about soft limbs and trembling flesh. *Even if that was the last thing in the world he wanted, or needed.* He felt his body tense in unwilling reaction to his vaguely erotic thoughts. 'I was hoping for someone a little more experienced,' he said harshly.

She heard the sudden censure in his voice and all Ashley's survival instincts came to the fore as she imagined being sacked from her job before she'd even started. She lifted her chin. 'Oh, I think you'll find I have plenty of experience for the kind of work you require, Mr Marchant.'

'Jack.'

'Jack,' she corrected.

'Someone more middle-aged, then,' he amended. 'Who won't mind locking herself away in this dark corner of the country.' He frowned. Had she idealised the job and the life she was going to find here? 'There aren't any nightclubs around here, you know. It's pretty quiet—more than quiet, in fact. No bright lights or big pubs crowded with young men.'

'I'm not really into nightclubs and bright lights.'

There was a pause as Jack's eyes narrowed. No. With that sensible hairstyle and that rather sensible sweater and skirt, he couldn't really imagine her gyrating in some sparkly little number on an overcrowded dance-floor. 'Well, I hope you aren't going to be bored.'

She shook her head, wondering if she had imagined some kind of dark warning in his voice. 'I doubt it. And eighteen isn't so young—not really.'

He gave a bitter laugh. 'Oh, believe me, it is,' he contradicted shortly, wondering if his own face ever looked as fresh as hers. Had his eyes ever been so clear and bright—so perfect and unlined? A long time ago, maybe. Before the army. Before... His mouth tightened. Before the random lottery of life had given him a one-way ticket to hell... He bent down to throw another log on the fire and it spurted into orange life. 'Once you've passed thirty-five—then someone of your age is pretty much in cradle-country.'

How old was *he*? Ashley mused in response. Thirty-five? Forty? His face wasn't particularly lined, but it had the shadows and furrows of experience etched deep into it. It suddenly occurred to her that if Jack Marchant decided that she wasn't what he wanted, then that would be that. There would be no job—and no roof over her head, either. And she *needed* the money—more than she'd ever needed money in her life. For him, her employment probably meant nothing, but for her it meant everything. Desperation made her argue her case—though some instinct told her not to show it.

'It's not as if there's something weird about working at this age,' she defended quietly. 'Though these days everybody seems to think there is. If you're old enough to vote, then surely you're old enough to go out to work.'

Unexpectedly, he found himself thinking how her face was completely transformed by her smile—and got the feeling she didn't do it very often. 'And you've worked since when?'

'Since I was sixteen.'

'Doing what?'

'Secretarial work, mainly—although I like to think I'm flexible enough to turn my hand to pretty much most things. My last job was in a boarding school. Before that I was in a hotel.'

'But always live-in jobs?'

'That's right. I'm hoping to save up for a deposit on my own place one day.' When she'd cleared the massive debt which hung like a heavy weight dangled over her head...

'And you had no desire to go to university?'

Ashley sighed, wondering why people always leapt to such predictable conclusions. Of course she'd *wanted* to go to university—but desire and feasibility were two entirely different things. Moving innumerable times in your formative years and attending some of the worst schools in the country did not tend to provide you with the kind of academic qualifications you needed to go to college.

'It just didn't work out that way,' she said quietly.

He heard the quiet defensiveness in her voice and something made him want to pursue it. 'No pushy parents?'

She swallowed. 'I have no parents.'

'No, I thought not,' he said softly.

Ashley stared at him. Was he some sort of mind-reader—or did she just carry an invisible aura about her which proclaimed 'orphan'? Her lips trembled. 'H-how?'

'Because there is something oddly self-contained about you,' he answered cryptically, thinking how innocent she looked when her lips shivered like that. 'Something which tells me you have been looking after yourself for a long time.'

'You are very perceptive,' she said slowly, almost to herself, and she saw his eyes narrow.

'I'm a writer,' he said mockingly. 'It goes with the territory. We may not be the best people at engaging in social niceties—but our observational skills are highly honed. Which is why I'd also hazard that you're a city girl?'

'Because I walk in lanes and scare the horses?'

'There's that of course. And by your pale face, which looks as if it has never seen sunshine,' he observed, finding his gaze drawn once more to her features. She was no beauty, that was for sure—and yet she had something which set her apart. Was it her eyes, which looked like a paintbox swirl of different greens? Or something about her quietness and watchful air? You didn't meet very many women with that rare air of containment, not these days. 'Very pale,' he finished slowly as an odd kind of lump rose in his throat.

And once again, Ashley felt a sudden sense of awareness begin to sizzle at her skin as his black eyes captured her in their gaze. The intimate flicker of the firelight seemed to have marooned them in their own private world where none of the usual rules seemed to apply. One where her new boss could study her as if she were beneath a microscope—and she would accept it as perfectly normal. She cleared her throat as she scrabbled round for something to break this oddly hypnotic and mesmerising mood.

'Did...' she hesitated '...did the hospital give you the all-clear?'

He raised his eyebrows. 'Why, do you think I have taken leave of my senses? That I'm speaking in a deranged way?'

'Since this is only the second time I've met you, it's far too early for me to make a judgement like that.'

At this Jack gave a low laugh and leaned further back into the cushions of the chair. So behind that demure, pale face she was capable of sarcasm, was she? Just as it seemed she was capable of answering his questions with an honesty which was as rare as it was disarming. Which would suggest she wasn't quite as mouselike as her appearance suggested. 'You'll have to let me know when you come to a verdict about my sanity,' he mocked softly.

Ashley bit back a smile. 'I don't actually think that's in my job specification.'

'Perhaps not.' He bent to toss another log into the smouldering fire. 'So what *did* the agency tell you about the job?'

He rested his hands against his chest as he waited for her answer—his fingers steepled together against the dark shadow of his jaw. The pose was faintly brooding—so that for a moment Ashley thought it looked as if he were holding an imaginary gun and the stark and unexpected metaphor unsettled her. She guessed that with his army experience, he was no stranger to guns and violence...

But more than anything, in that moment, Jack Marchant looked all dark and rampant sexuality. Like every woman's fantasy come to life. Suddenly, she understood why middle-aged Julia at the agency had become hot and flustered when she'd described Jack Marchant as 'formidable'. And maybe his effect on women didn't have an age barrier—because suddenly she was feeling a little hot and flustered herself.

'I...they said you'd written several biographies of great men. Mainly military men.'

'How very dry that sounds.'

'And that I would be typing up your latest manuscript—'

'From longhand? I hope they specified that? I've tried typing it myself but tapping out on a keyboard distracts my thoughts. I prefer to write it out—and I don't think I'm alone in that.' He looked at her curiously. 'Many authors still do, I believe?'

Ashley nodded. She found herself wondering what his handwriting was like. As torturous and as twisted as the thought processes which seemed to be firing up behind those ebony eyes? 'So I believe.'

'And they told you it's a novel?'

'Yes.'

'Have you ever typed a novel before?'

She nodded. 'I did one by Hannah Minnock early last year—she was a teacher at the school where I was working and it was her first book, called *Ringing The*

Changes. It was a chick-lit book.' His face remained blank. 'You know—funny, frothy stuff aimed at professional women. About divorce.'

His eyes narrowed. 'And that's considered *funny*, is it?'

'I just type the story,' she said stiffly. 'I don't sit there in judgement of it.'

'Well, you'll find that my novel is as far removed from your frothy, fluffy "chick-lit" book as it is possible to be.'

'I rather thought it might be,' she answered quietly. 'What exactly is it about?'

There was a pause and, briefly, she saw his knuckles tightening and the flicker of the flames casting bloodlike shadows over them. 'My time in the army.'

'Oh, I see.'

'Really?' He raised his dark brows in mocking question. 'And what exactly do you know about army life?'

'Well, only what I've seen on the news and read in the papers.'

'And are you easily shocked? Are you queasy about blood and gore?' Black eyes blazed at her and sent out an unmistakable challenge. 'Do you scare easily, Ashley?'

She felt the sudden race of her heart in response to his question. Once, she would have blurted out that yes, she had known fear—real fear. The cruel personality of one of her foster mothers had seen to that. Sadistic Mrs Fraser who had locked her in the cupboard under the stairs all evening after accusing her of a crime of which the ten-year-old Ashley had been innocent.

She would never forget the experience—not as long as she lived. It had left a hideous mark on her memory which could never be erased. The dust and the cobwebs which had tickled her cheeks had been bad enough— taunting her with the knowledge that large, wriggly spiders were probably just waiting to drop down onto her head. But it had been the darkness which had terrified her more than anything. The claustrophobic darkness which had provided an ideal breeding ground for her fevered imagination. Ghosts and ghouls had come to haunt her that night and visions of lonely graveyards had filled her with an unspeakable kind of dread.

When eventually the door had been opened and light had flooded in Ashley had been beyond comprehension—or past caring. Her lips had been bleeding from where she had clamped her teeth into them and her clothes had been damp with sweat. The doctor told her afterwards that she must have had some kind of fit—but she would never forget the look of horror on his face, which he hadn't quite managed to hide. As if he couldn't believe what he was seeing—as if such things shouldn't be happening in this modern day and age. But they did happen. Ashley had never been under any illusion about that. Times changed but human nature didn't.

The council had found another placement for her almost immediately—although Mrs Fraser had used her clever and manipulative tongue to convince her next set of foster parents that she was nothing but trouble.

A liar and a cheat, she'd said. Ashley's reputation had preceded her. She had quickly learned that if someone had a fixed idea that you were a bad person, then they would be on the lookout for signs to prove just that.

As a result, she had learned to subdue her hot temper and quick tongue. She had buried her more excitable character traits along with the squalid memory of that day. She had become quiet and calm Ashley, who would not rise to provocation or threat. And if Jack Marchant wanted to know the precise details of when and why she had been scared—then he would wait in vain for an answer from her. Because some secrets were best forgotten…

'No, I don't scare easily,' she said.

'Don't you? And yet just now I saw something darken your eyes,' he observed softly. 'Something which looked exactly like fear.'

He was, she realised, an exceedingly perceptive man. And surely too intelligent to accept a smooth evasion? But he was her employer, nothing else. He had rights, yes—but only those which affected her work. He did not have the right to probe into her past and to prise out the horrors which she had buried so deep. She lifted her chin to meet the question in his eyes. 'Everyone has dark corners in their memories—things they'd rather just forget,' she said quietly. 'Don't they?'

Her words produced a change in *him*. Ashley saw the flicker of a pulse at his temple and a fleeting expression of anguish which briefly darkened his craggy face. It was strange seeing so powerful a man look almost…

almost *despairing*, but the look was gone so quickly that she wondered if she might have imagined it.

Instead, he gave that odd smile which curved the edges of his hard lips and didn't really seem to have any humour in it. 'Let's leave my memories out of it, shall we?' he said, his dismissive tone indicating that the conversation was at an end—and then he rose to his feet as if to reinforce it. 'Come on, let's go and eat supper.'

He looked down into her upturned face, towering over her and somehow making her feel very small and fragile. Ashley felt the surface of her skin icing, her skin turning to goose-bumps as his tall body bathed her in its dark shadow.

Because never had a man's harsh and enigmatic expression made her feel quite so unsettled.

CHAPTER THREE

ASHLEY had a restless first night at Blackwood. The branches battering at the windows kept sleep at bay and so did the images which burned into her memory every time she shut her eyes. Images of raven hair, burnished by firelight. Of a towering physique and a powerful body. And more than anything—of a cold and intelligent gaze which seemed to slice right through her like an icy blast of winter wind.

She and Jack Marchant had eaten supper together, but as soon as the meal was finished he had excused himself and disappeared into his study to work, closing the door behind him. Leaving Ashley feeling alone and out of place in the vast downstairs of the house. She'd escaped to her own room, where she took a bath and washed her hair—before lying awake and restless in bed and wondering if she was going to be happy here. And the worst thing of all was that she couldn't seem to shake the image of Jack from her mind.

Jack in denim, having fallen from his horse—his face twisted in pain and his raven hair all windswept.

Jack in a silk shirt and tapered trousers—so imposing and aristocratic as he sat beside the fire, with the flames dancing shadows all over his rugged features.

And just one floor beneath her Jack was in bed. Was he naked beneath linen sheets as fine as the ones in which she herself lay? Did that powerful body toss and turn as hers did? Her cheeks burning as she acknowledged her uncharacteristically erotic thoughts, Ashley buried her face in the welcome cool of the pillow.

Eventually, she drifted off to sleep—only to be woken with a start by the distant sound of a door slamming and then the beginning of a rhythm which confused her at first but was unmistakable once she'd worked out what it was. In the darkness, Ashley frowned.

It was the sound of somebody pacing the floor.

Quickly, she sat up in bed, her eyes growing accustomed to the faint light in the room. Surely Jack Marchant was not an insomniac? And yet who else could it be making those agitated footsteps—when the two of them were alone in the house?

Listening to the sound of heavy pacing, she found herself wondering what thoughts were going through his head—and what could possibly keep a man like that awake at night.

After that, sleep became impossible and she gave up trying to chase it, and she lay there until some ancient central-heating system began to crank into life and herald the start of another day. Eventually she saw the first pale rays of light as they crept through a sliver of space between the curtains.

The room was chilly and swiftly she jumped out of bed and dressed in jeans and layers of warm clothing, before slipping down the sweeping staircase, listening out for signs that Jack might be awake and ready to start work. But the house was in complete silence and, after putting on her sturdy shoes, she let herself out of the kitchen door and went outside, where a fairy-tale landscape awaited her.

During the night a heavy frost had fallen—transforming the bleak, grey landscape of yesterday into one brushed by pure white. The garden looked like an old black and white photo with each blade of grass and every branch painted in monochrome.

For a moment she just stood there, revelling in the unfamiliar country scene and thinking that it looked like the picture on the front of a Christmas card. There was always something so pure about the frost—it was as white as snow and yet somehow more stark and understated. Less showy. Lifting her hand, she ran a questing finger along a branch and felt it shower down over her head—like fine snowflakes. A sudden sense of exhilaration filled her as she began to walk along the frozen path, enjoying the fresh air and space of the countryside and thinking how *quiet* it was when compared to the city.

And then something intruded into her consciousness—some slight movement which must have registered at the corner of her eye. Looking up towards the manor house, she felt her heart skip a beat because there—framed by a curved gothic window and silhouetted like some towering statue—stood the dark and brooding figure of Jack Marchant. He was completely still, as motionless as if he were part of the house itself and yet, even from this distance, Ashley could feel the icy burn of his eyes as he watched her.

She felt her heart miss a beat. Had he gone looking for her—eager to start work—only to find her strolling around the grounds, running her fingertips over frost-glazed branches like a simple fool?

She hurried back towards the house, hoping to be able to tidy herself and be installed ready to start work before he came downstairs. But she hoped in vain, for she opened the kitchen door to the gentle hiss of a coffee machine and the comforting smell of toast.

Jack was standing there, his strong hands cupped around a steaming mug as he stared out of the window over the kitchen garden. For a moment, she stood and drank in the view, taken aback by the domesticity of the scene—and by the infinitely more disturbing image of his hard, high buttocks encased in faded denim. His bare feet gripped the cool grey flagstones and his dark hair curled over the edge of his collar.

She had never seen a man in such an intimate setting before and it made her feel acutely self-conscious. Ashley swallowed, trying to clamp down her rising excitement and the sudden frisson which skittered over her skin. There seemed something almost indecent about the sight of his toes and the unexpected glimpse of bare flesh. The warmth of the kitchen was seductive—but not nearly as seductive as the hard gleam from his eyes as he turned to look at her. Did he notice the sudden tremble of her mouth, and wonder what on earth had caused it?

'Good morning,' she said, a touch breathlessly.

'Ashley.' He said her name softly as he saw the high rise of colour to her cheeks and the way her hair spilled down over her shoulders this morning. Her lips gleamed where she must have licked them and he found himself wondering what it would be like to kiss them, even as he acknowledged how impossibly young she looked. 'Are you always up so early, taking walks?'

Still feeling a little light-headed, she shook her head. 'Not really. The last place I was living in wasn't really the kind of place you'd go out walking—not at any time of the day. But as I was awake…' She peeled off her frosty coat and thought how tired he looked. His features were strained with fatigue and his black eyes were shadowed by blue smudges beneath.

'Sit down,' he said.

'Thanks.' Something about the way he was looking at her was making her feel ridiculously weak and she was grateful to be able to slide into one of the chairs which surrounded the scrubbed oak table.

'Did you sleep well?' he questioned suddenly.

She hesitated. She supposed she could lie and tell the polite fib. But what would be the point? Surely he must have realised that she'd heard him as he had paced the corridors? 'Not terribly well, no.'

'Oh? Did something keep you awake?'

His voice was studiedly casual but she felt torn as

she met the question in his eyes. If she lied, simply to gloss over things—mightn't that enrage him and make him think that he couldn't trust her to tell the truth? And wasn't honesty important to her—more important to her than pretty much anything else? 'Actually, I heard footsteps. Pacing the corridor.'

For a split second his face darkened and Ashley felt a moment of disquiet as she looked at him. Maybe she shouldn't have mentioned it after all. But just as quickly the look had gone and was replaced by one of curiosity.

'So were you afraid that the house was haunted?' he questioned silkily. 'The tormented spirit of one of my ancestors, perhaps.' He poured coffee into a mug and pushed it across the table towards her. 'Do you believe in ghosts, Ashley?'

She shook her head. She thought he was trying to change the subject and she wondered why. 'No. No, I don't.'

Like a croupier, he directed the sugar bowl in her direction, bringing it to a halt when she shook her head. 'Or did you think it was me?'

'I knew it was you.' Her heart missed a beat as she met the question in his narrowed eyes. 'How...I mean, how could it *not* be you—when we're the only two people in the house?'

Jack's mouth hardened. He wondered what she had done when she'd heard him. Had she lain there and wondered whether he might sleepwalk his way into her room by mistake?

With a sudden and inexplicable clarity, he almost wished he had—as he pictured her slender frame beneath the outline of a thin sheet. He could imagine pulling the sheet aside to see a slender, coltish body—her curving breasts topped with rosy nipples. Could imagine those unpainted lips of hers framing themselves into a silent question as he sought the comfort and warmth of her fragile body. He swallowed as he imagined sliding his hand between soft thighs and gently parting them. Was he going out of his *mind*? Abruptly, he sat down at the table, glad to be able to conceal his aching groin. He drank some too-hot coffee and winced, glad for its scalding distraction. 'And were you frightened?'

She picked up her mug and shrugged. 'I try not to do fear.'

Something about her quiet response impressed him. He watched her as she sat there in his kitchen, hair still damp from the frost that had fallen on her head, and he found himself thinking how difficult it must be for her to be catapulted into his life. To just turn up at a place like this, not knowing what, or who, she would find. To have to blend in and mould herself to what was expected of her. 'What makes someone like you take on this sort of job?' he questioned suddenly.

His question was so unexpected that Ashley didn't have one of her stock answers ready—about liking variety in her work and wanting to get as many different kinds of work experience as possible. Because if the truth were known she wouldn't really have opted for a post which took her away from all her friends, to a deserted part of a bleak, northern moorland in the middle of January.

'I need the money,' she said starkly.

He raised his eyebrows by a fraction—because most people hid this kind of truth behind a casual lie or exaggeration. 'Why?'

Ashley shrugged, wondering whether it was the directness of his question or that searching onyx stare which made her want to tell him. Or was it simply the realisation that here was not a man who could be fobbed off with flimsy excuses? Would he be shocked by the truth? 'I'm in debt.'

'Oh, dear.' There was a pause. 'By much?'

She supposed it wouldn't be much to him. 'Enough.'

'I see.' Thoughtfully, he sipped at his coffee. 'So what caused it—was it extravagance, or necessity?'

This time, Ashley chose her words carefully—because what would someone like Jack Marchant know about the realities of her life and trying to manage a budget when money was tight? When an unexpected bill could send your bank balance plummeting and then other expenses showered in on top to add to the mounting pressure. That was the trouble with debt—somehow you never quite caught up with yourself. It happened to other people her age but most of them had parents they could turn to if they were desperate. Someone who might be able to help them out with a short-term loan. But she'd never had anybody to run to.

'Necessity,' she said. 'Too many bills arrived all at

the same time—and then a couple of unexpected ones only added to the burden.'

'I see,' said Jack.

'I mean, it wasn't shoes or a designer coat,' she added quickly. 'I didn't have an urge to go off on an exotic foreign holiday, or anything like that.'

'No. I can't imagine that it was,' he concurred, because somehow he couldn't imagine her having expensive tastes or lusting after fine clothes. Not judging by what she wore—rather plain and ordinary clothes, which nonetheless did little to hide the fact that there was a very nubile body beneath them. He wondered what it must be like to have to count and account for every penny as he acknowledged how difficult it must be for someone like Ashley Jones to survive. And unexpectedly, he felt a sudden pang of compassion. 'Well, you should be able to save most of your salary here,' he said gruffly. 'Since there's not really a lot to spend it on in the middle of the moors.'

'No, I guess there isn't,' she said quietly, his attitude surprising her—making her think that perhaps he wasn't all he seemed. He might be a powerful and wealthy landowner who'd never had to worry about bills, but he wasn't being judgemental about *her* situation. In fact, he had sounded really quite *kind*, she realised, with a small glow of pleasure.

'Anyway,' he said hastily as he became aware that he'd made her blush and that her cheeks were flaring rose-pink. It was a long time since he had made a woman blush and the last time it had happened had been in *very* different circumstances. Feeling another unwanted jerk of desire, he felt a stab of irritation. What he did *not* need was for her to start coming over all girly. For her face to start colouring every time he spoke to her, drawing attention to the fact that she was young and firm and that, despite the relative plainness of her face, he had seen her lips tremble. And didn't nature make young women's lips tremble to make you wonder what it must be like to kiss them? 'Help yourself to breakfast,' he said hurriedly. 'And by the time you've eaten, we'll be ready to start work. Okay?'

'Okay,' she agreed, her eyes following him as he walked out of the kitchen.

She nibbled at some toast and marmalade and when she'd finished she stacked the dishwasher and stopped to freshen up on her way to Jack's office. Usually, Ashley didn't have a trace of vanity in her nature, but this morning something made her linger for a moment by the mirror in the cloakroom. As if she wanted to see herself as *he* had seen her—but not wanting to wonder why.

The unremarkable oval of her face was reflected back at her as she pushed her hair back behind her ears. It was easy to be critical of her looks—as so many people had been over the years—and the foster mothers who had been looking for a doll-like accessory had been the worst. Little girls were supposed to be cute and pretty, but Ashley had never been that. Her skin was too pale and her mouth much too wide for her face. Yes, she'd been blessed with thick hair, but she realised that the neat, restrained style she wore for work gave her a rather *stern* appearance. Undoubtedly, her eyes were her best feature—for they were large and green—and this morning they were shining more brightly than usual.

Was that because she'd just drunk coffee with a ruggedly gorgeous man who had been unexpectedly kind and thus made her look up to him in a way he'd probably never intended? And didn't that say something about her—that deep down she didn't know how to talk to an attractive man without reading too much into it?

She finished drying her hands. Well, she didn't need to read too much into it. Clearly, Jack Marchant wasn't judging her negatively because she'd got herself into debt—but neither was he going to give her another thought. He certainly wasn't interested in what she looked like—why, a man like that could have his pick of any woman he wanted! So she'd better just do what she was being paid to do and knuckle down to her job— instead of threatening her livelihood with emotional sensitivity and uncharacteristic bouts of studying her appearance.

After running upstairs to quickly change and weave her hair into its habitual twist, she hurried along to the study which he'd briefly shown her before dinner last night, relieved to find it empty—giving her the chance to acquaint herself with it before he arrived. But it wasn't like any other office she'd ever seen. It was a pristinely tidy room and completely devoid of any of the usual knick-knacks which most people used to personalise their working space.

There were no photos. No foreign artefacts to remind

him of long-ago holidays or tours of duty when he'd been in the army. No medals or commendations. No tarnished trophies showing earlier sporting triumphs. Only row upon row of books lined the walls—mainly histories and biographies—all beautifully bound in soft, toiled leather. Other than this, there was no evidence of his past—or, indeed, anything of his present life. They said you could tell what someone was like by their surroundings, but if that were the case then Jack Marchant could be classed as something of an enigma.

In fact, the only thing which drew her eye was an exquisite little wooden cabinet which was tucked away in the corner of the room. Its gleaming walnut surface was inlaid with mother-of-pearl and was so beautiful that she wondered why it was hidden away like this.

She ran her fingers over the smooth wood and irresistibly they strayed to the single drawer—which slid out as smoothly as a hot knife being removed from butter. Glancing down, she saw a woman's silken scarf in deep azure-blue. It was the last thing she had expected to find. Shot with delicate strands of gold, it reminded her of sunlight in a cloudless blue sky and Ashley blinked in surprise. Whose scarf was *that*? she wondered—just as the sound of footsteps along the corridor announced Jack's return. Quickly, she slid shut the drawer and stepped away from the cabinet.

At that moment he came into the room, carrying a thick sheaf of papers, and his eyes narrowed when he saw her. 'What are you doing?' he demanded.

Ashley was an honest person but she was also an

instinctive one—and she valued her livelihood too much to risk it by admitting that what she'd been doing could be considered as snooping, and she certainly hadn't meant to do *that*. 'Nothing,' she said quickly, quashing her curiosity. 'Just…just looking around the place and trying to get my bearings. And I'm ready to start work when you are.'

For a moment, his black eyes remained trained on her and the hard light at their depths glittered like jet. The kindness and warmth he'd displayed in the kitchen seemed to have completely evaporated, she thought, with a rising feeling of panic. His face was back to being formidable and he was now regarding her with cold detachment.

'By the way, you've signed a confidentiality agreement, haven't you, Ashley?' he questioned silkily.

She lifted her eyes to his and forced a smile. It wasn't an unreasonable question for an employer to ask in the circumstances—though it seemed to emphasise the fact that she was nothing more than his subordinate. ' Yes,' she said quietly. 'I have.'

But oddly enough, the question hurt far more than it should have done.

CHAPTER FOUR

No MORE was said about confidentiality agreements. And Ashley didn't mention the beautiful scarf she had found tucked away in the bureau. She didn't dare. It was none of her business—and there was something about Jack Marchant's demeanour which seemed to discourage the asking of questions. Unless he was the one doing the asking, of course.

If only it were as easy to brush aside the growing complexity of her feelings for him and the confusion she felt as a result of them. She wondered what on earth she had thought about before she'd started working for Jack. When had he started to occupy most of the space inside her head? And what had happened to make her become so fascinated by him?

Whenever he walked into the room—whether he was wearing his beautifully cut more formal clothes or the faded denim which suited him just as much—she couldn't seem to tear her eyes away from him. Unnoticed, she found herself gazing at his rugged pro-file when his attention was absorbed by something he was reading. Sometimes, he would look up and catch her watching him—and so, of course, she forced herself to look away, her cheeks burning, terrified that her eyes might give away all her inappropriate feelings. Sometimes he would stand close to her and her senses felt as if they were being assaulted by his proximity. Her breath would catch in her dry throat so that even breathing became difficult when he was around.

Why was she reacting this way to a man who would never be anything more than an employer to her? Who probably viewed her in exactly the same way as he did Christine, his housekeeper—or the cleaners who came in several times a week to keep his manor house gleaming. How absolutely horrified he would be to learn that she sometimes lay awake in bed at night—alerted by the sound of his own sleeplessness—wondering what it would be like to be made love to by a man like Jack Marchant.

One morning he stopped in front of her desk, his tall shadow enveloping her. She looked up into the jet gleam of his eyes and felt the automatic quickening of her heart. *Don't react*, she told herself fiercely. *Don't let him see that you're acutely aware of him as a man, rather than a boss.*

'G-good morning, Jack.'

'Good morning, Ashley.'

Curving her lips into a pleasant smile, she tilted her head in question, wishing that he would move away a little—at least far enough for her not to have to inhale his delicious raw scent. 'Can I do something for you?'

For a moment Jack silently cursed her innocent question. *Could she do something for him?* She most certainly could. He wondered if she had any idea of the thoughts which instantly came blazing into his imagination and tried to imagine her shock if he were to express them. Thoughts which began with a sudden and inexplicable kiss and ended with him thrusting deep inside her slender body and seeing that calm smile of hers dissolving into out-of-control pleasure. Erotic and distracting thoughts he should *not* have been having about his secretary. Not in any circumstances, but especially not in his own particular circumstances... And weren't matters being made worse by her unique attitude towards him?

He gave a ragged sigh. Ashley was the least provocative woman he'd ever met—and as a consequence he wasn't quite sure how to deal with her. If she'd been batting eyelids heavy with mascara and bursting out of skin-tight clothes, handling her would have been a piece of cake. He knew plenty of women like that. Just as he knew how to deal with their sexual voracity. The trouble was that he felt completely wrong footed by someone who was so damned *sweet*.

Yet Jack was no fool—and he certainly didn't aspire to false modesty. He knew desire when he saw it, and he'd surprised it in the darkening of her big green eyes on more than one occasion. Some women might not have bothered if he'd noticed them self-consciously biting their lips when he looked at them—in fact, they might have hoped that he would capitalise on it. But

Ashley was the opposite. She was doing her damndest to hide her feelings from him and conversely that was just making him want her *more*. Her studied modesty and the distance she was trying to put between them was an unexpected turn-on. A big turn-on. And he wasn't quite sure what he intended to do about it…

'I just wondered,' he said huskily, 'how it was going.'

'Going?' Confused, Ashley stopped typing and stared up into his face, steeling herself against the dark gleam in his eyes. 'The…book, you mean?'

'No, that's not what I mean—I can see for myself that you're making good progress.' He gave a half-impatient wave of his hand at the neat pile of paper beside her. ' I meant, your life here—generally. Your salary. That kind of thing.'

Despite the sudden drying of her mouth, Ashley bit back a smile. He made it sound as if he were asking a battalion of his troops whether they were satisfied with their rations! The requisite pep talk for the staff. *Because that's all you are to him*, she reminded herself. 'It's fine. Honestly. It's more than fine.'

'You're not bored?'

'I try never to be bored, Jack.'

'I'm very pleased to hear it. I always think that boredom indicates a lack of imagination.' He stared into her wide-spaced eyes—as lush and green as any spring meadow. 'No complaints with the way you're being treated?'

Complaints? She stared up into his piercing black

eyes. Not exactly *complaints*, more like frustrations, a whole litany of them—all of them minor and none that she would ever dare express to *him*. Because there wasn't an employment tribunal in the land which would uphold her protest of having a too-sexy boss.

As happened with all jobs, she'd quickly settled into a routine. She'd soon got used to the big house and the fact that her meals were cooked for her—and that the cleaners changed her sheets and left a little vase of flowers on the window sill. Just as she got used to the dramatic landscape outside her window and working for an enormously wealthy landowner. But working for Jack was different from anything she'd ever done before and that was everything to do with him. Because she'd never been attracted to any of her bosses before. It was unprofessional—and Ashley tried very hard not to *do* unprofessional. But it wasn't easy—not when every day she was shoehorned into close proximity with him.

And Jack Marchant would tempt a saint.

It wasn't just his iron-hard physique—which had been honed during his army years and had stayed with him ever since. Nor was it his ruggedly handsome face— which could veer so distractingly between forbidding and animated. No, Ashley decided—it was every part of him. The mocking sense of humour. The keen intelligence. The occasional glimpse of understanding—like the day she'd told him about her financial predicament.

Yet she suspected that there was a side of himself which he kept hidden away—and which made him so much of an enigma. The inner disquiet which seemed to burn within him—which made her heart want to reach out to him and to ask what troubled him. He *must* be troubled—for why else would she hear his footsteps pacing the floor in the dead of night?

She would lie there, listening and trying to imagine what had caused it. Was he aware that his tread on the wooden corridors always woke her—and that she lay there longing to go down and comfort him? But the subject had never been brought up again. Not after that first time when he had asked her if she believed in ghosts. And it wasn't the kind of thing you could just casually mention over morning coffee...

Sometimes he ate with her and sometimes she ate alone—picking at the delicious food which Christine prepared and served in the room they called the Garden Room. Jack told her that he wanted to make the most of the daylight hours, which were so short in winter, so he gave her every afternoon off and they would resume work at four, once the light had begun to fade, and then would carry on until just before dinner.

After lunch each day, he would disappear to the stables to ride his horse and Ashley would wrap up warmly to walk round the estate—revelling in the wildness of the distant moorlands and aware of the beauty of her surroundings in a way she'd never been before. Was that Jack's influence too, she wondered—that somehow, subtly, he seemed to have awoken all her senses?

But one day, he turned up late for the meal and spent most of it scowling. Ashley watched as he picked up a decanter and poured himself half a glass of claret and sipped it. He *never* drank at lunchtime!

'Is something wrong?' she ventured eventually.

His eyes met hers over the rim of the glass. 'There's no riding today.'

'Oh? Why's that?'

'Nero is ill.'

'Oh, dear—not badly, I hope?'

'No. Not badly.' He shook his head slightly impatiently. 'The vet's been over to see him—given him an injection and told the stable-girl to make sure he's kept warm and dry. He's supposed to rest for the next few days.'

'Well, that's all right, then.' Ashley smiled in what she hoped was a placating manner—because he seemed in a very peculiar mood. 'He'll soon be better and then you can start riding him again.'

'Yes.' He put the crystal glass down heavily on the table. But it wasn't all right. It was frustrating. Damn it—*everything* was frustrating. He looked forward to his afternoon exercise, revelling in the sense of freedom and power it gave him as he and the animal thundered over the moorland. And Jack was aware that it was more than a love of all things equine which had recently made his daily ride seem more vital than usual. He knew that he was using the exercise to sublimate the growing hunger he felt for Ashley. A sexual hunger which was as inappropriate as it was forbidden.

His body tense, he stood up, feeling the heavy beat of his heart as he stared down at her. How was it possible that this artless little thing should have heated his blood and invaded his imagination so that his eyes wanted to drink her in every time she walked into his study? Had he *misjudged* her innocence? Was she perhaps perfectly aware that she was driving him crazy with desire?

Ashley met the ebony glitter of his eyes as he loomed over the debris of their meal, wondering why his face had darkened so that he was looking at her almost *angrily*. 'Never mind,' she said lightly. 'If you like, we could carry on working. The story's just reached an interesting part—but you've done more than your usual amount of crossing-outs and alterations and it's probably best if I checked with you as I went along.'

'No,' he said suddenly. 'You don't need to do that. I'm fed up with the damned book. You've worked hard all morning and you deserve a break. I need the fresh air and so do you. Let's go for a walk instead.'

'A walk?'

'There's no need to sound so shocked, Ashley,' he grated. 'You walk every day after lunch, don't you?'

'Well, yes, I do.' She looked at him doubtfully— suddenly nervous and wanting to throw obstacles in the way, without being really sure why. 'But I...I don't walk very quickly.'

'Then I'll make allowances for you—and it isn't some kind of race. Now, go get your coat,' he said, in the kind of tone which brooked no argument.

Ashley went into the hall and began tying up the laces of her walking shoes. Why on earth did he want to go walking with her? she wondered, her fingers annoyingly shaky as she pulled a woollen beanie onto her head, before going outside to find him waiting. And why was he in such a filthy temper?

He was standing beneath the oak which dominated the far side of the lawn. It was a mighty specimen— he'd told her himself that it was over a century old, with huge, curved branches which looked like powerful limbs. And yet somehow he was more than a match for the magnificent tree—as if nature had suddenly decided to showcase two examples of her finest handiwork, side by side. Ashley found her lips drying as she looked at him, the heavy thunder of her heart hinting at danger.

'Where do you want to go?' he questioned as she approached.

'I don't mind,' she said awkwardly, digging her hands deep into the pockets of her coat. 'Don't you have a favourite walk of your own?'

'Of course I do. But I want to know yours.'

She turned to look up at the smoky grey clouds which were puffing through the sky—suddenly envying that cloud its freedom to float high above the world and all its cares. 'I think I'd like to go up that hill at the back of the house—right to the very top. You know—the bit where you get the best view of the moors.'

'I know it very well,' he said softly.

They set off. The ground was soft and sank beneath their feet and it made the walk seem slightly tougher than usual. Ashley was fit, but unusually she was a little out of breath by the time she reached the top of the incline. Or maybe that was because Jack's legs were long—so much longer than hers—so that they seemed to eat up the ground in front of him.

It felt strange to be out alone with him in the great outdoors like this—but it only added to the confused swirl of her thoughts. It made her feel as if they were a *couple.* As if she had been born to walk with a man like Jack Marchant—enjoying the comfortable ease of their shared silence and seeing his dark, craggy profile etched against the stark landscape. Yet they were only here because his horse was sick—because Jack had asked her on a whim. No point reading any more into it than that.

He stopped when they reached the highest point—and Ashley stood beside him—acknowledging with guilty pleasure how tiny he made her feel. And how fragile. Her limbs seemed so slight when compared with his— because even his thick coat couldn't disguise the dormant strength which lay beneath.

Oh, why was she thinking this way—risking making herself a laughing stock—an illegitimate orphan from the wrong sides of the track, nurturing a passion for a man who was way out of her reach?

With an effort, she forced her attention away from his profile to stare at the scene in front of her. From here you could see Blackwood Manor as well as the rugged beauty of the moorland beyond. It was always a stunning view—but it was harsh and uncompromising, too. Had this craggy landscape helped make him the man he was? A man about whom she still knew very little, she realised—despite their forced proximity.

'Have you always lived here?' she questioned.

There was silence for a moment, and then he shrugged.

'Until I went away to school. Then university. And then the army, of course.'

'The army must have been very tough.' Embarrassed now, she shrugged her shoulders. 'I'm sorry—that sounds like a stupid platitude. Of course it was tough. I just...just never realised how much until I starting reading your book.'

'It's a novel, Ashley,' he said gently.

'I know it is.' The words came out in a rush, before she could stop them. 'But that bit...the bit where the officer is out in the desert and gets out of the car and when he turns back, he...he...' Her sentence faded but she knew that his powerful description was vividly in both their minds. The flash of a bomb. Bright light and a sickening sound. And through the dull muffle of temporary deafness—the senses returning just when you didn't want them to. Smelling the burning of flesh and hearing the gasps of the dying—and the sight of carnage all around you. 'He's...he's you, isn't he?'

His mouth hardened. 'Why, Ashley? Is it relevant?'

She heard the sudden harshness in his voice and wished she could have bitten back her words. 'Not—not really, I guess.'

'My past is irrelevant,' he growled. 'Everyone's is. This moment is all that any of us ever have. Understand? That there's no point looking back and remembering.

We can't change anything we've done—we just have to live with it.'

'Yes,' she answered quietly—because that was something she *did* understand. Because wouldn't she go crazy if she allowed herself to remember all the hard times of her childhood? 'I guess you're right.'

How calm her voice sounded, he thought. It was like balm poured onto his troubled spirit. He looked down into her face and suddenly his heart turned over. 'Do you realise that your features look perfect against this winter landscape?' he questioned suddenly. 'Your skin pale as snow—and your hair the colour of the bare earth.'

Ashley started as she searched his face for signs of mockery, but she could find none—only a kind of dark intensity about him which made him look so *alive*. As if in that snapshot moment he found her the single most alluring person in the world. And she wasn't imagining it—she definitely wasn't—because the tension was so palpable that she could have reached out and touched it.

For one snatched second, she allowed herself the forbidden fantasy she'd entertained over and over again. Of Jack pulling her into his arms and crushing her against his hard and powerful body. For hadn't she played out that scene countless times in her head as she lay in bed every night listening to his footsteps? Of him lowering his dark, rugged face to kiss her. Those black eyes gleaming some evocative message before his sensual lips came down to cover hers…

With a fierce determination, she forced the image from her mind. He was her *boss* and she needed this job. Needed it badly enough not to risk jeopardising it with *anything*.

'We'd...we'd better get back,' she stammered, and yet her legs felt as if they were rooted to the spot and she'd never be able to move again.

'Why?'

She raised her eyes up to his. 'Because—'

'Because of this?' Without warning, he pulled her into his arms, expelling a shuddering breath as he felt that first collision with her soft body. 'This damned thing between us which won't seem to go away?'

'Jack!'

'Jack, what?' he taunted.

All she could see was the sudden flintiness of his eyes—and the cold glint of pain at their depths. And she thought to herself, *Surely a man shouldn't look like this just before he kisses you?*

'Jack, we mustn't,' she whispered.

'Oh, but we must,' he negated harshly, compelled by something far stronger than reason or the sudden frantic clamour of his conscience. 'Because I think I'm going to go crazy unless we do.'

Some instinct told her to pull away from him but she couldn't. Because by then it was too late. By then he was moulding her even closer, so that she could feel the contours of his hard body against hers. Cupping her face between his hands, he stared down at her—his face a dark mask, looking for all the world like a man who had just seen a tortured image of his own future.

And then—just like all her forbidden fantasies—Jack Marchant bent his head and began to kiss her.

CHAPTER FIVE

JACK's lips crushed down on Ashley's, his kiss deep and passionate as his tongue probed deep inside her mouth. He groaned as he kissed her, making a sound of such helpless pleasure that Ashley made an answering moan of her own. She felt her hands grope blindly for his shoulders—as if she might slide to the ground without his support.

Her blood sang and her heart pounded. How shockingly intimate that felt. Jack's tongue inside her mouth. Jack pressing her against his body. Jack pressing his hips into hers with blatant desire. Her fingers bit into his heavy coat as she clutched onto him—and now his kiss became even more fervent.

He plundered her mouth without restraint, like a man who had tasted food after a long period of starvation. His hands moved to her hair, his fingers impatiently weaving through the carefully positioned pins, so that several strands began to tumble down around her face. She could feel the mad quickening of her heart and the strange, honeyed sensation which was making her body seem hot and tender and tight and restless—all at the same time. Like a coiled spring which was slowly beginning to unfurl.

He pulled her even nearer, so that the physique she had secretly admired from afar was now moulded firmly against her. And despite the clothing he wore she was acutely aware of his rampant masculinity—of the growing need at the very cradle of his body. It should have been daunting, and on one level it was—and yet on another it felt as if her entire life had been spent waiting for this moment.

'Ashley!' He whispered into her mouth and she gave an instinctive little mew of pleasure in response. She could feel the warmth of his breath mingling with hers and smell his masculine scent invading her nostrils.

'J-Jack,' she breathed—and then said it again, as if to reassure herself that she wasn't dreaming. 'Jack.'

'Yes,' he said unsteadily. 'Yes.'

Reaching down, he began to unbutton her coat, slipping his hand inside to cup one breast over her sweater, and Ashley jerked with shock and pleasure at the unexpected intimacy. Beneath the cheap wool, she felt her flesh swell and become acutely sensitive beneath his seeking fingers. And then he moved his hand, sliding it underneath the sweater to alight on her bra itself.

His fingers had now encountered a painfully tight nipple and were rubbing at it deliciously through the lace of her bra and Ashley found her senses clamouring to have him remove the obstruction. To have his whole hand cup the exquisitely aching mound. She could feel her nipple pushing painfully against the lace—as if her bra had suddenly become several sizes too small.

'Jack,' she moaned.

'You like that, don't you?' he whispered.

'Oh, yes. Yes.' She'd never felt like this before—never had a man touch her like this before. For several seconds she allowed the strange, sweet sensation to wash over her and felt the rush of desire which was spiralling up inside her. She registered her sudden urgent need for something more and allowed herself to wriggle restlessly in his arms.

'Please,' she heard herself whisper, as if someone had planted the word inside her mouth. 'Please keep doing that.'

'My pleasure,' he ground out.

No. It was her pleasure. *Hers.* She'd never thought that her body could feel like this. As if it were on fire—and only Jack could extinguish that fire. She met the urgent thrust of his hips with an instinctive one of her own—until reality hit her like a ton of bricks dropped from a great height and smashed into her thoughts.

She was standing on a bleak and barren moor, letting her boss make love to her!

Her breath coming in ragged little gasps, she tore herself out of his arms and stared up at his face—where another shock awaited her. For this was Jack Marchant as she had never seen him before, his features all dark and saturnine—looking like the devil himself. This was no longer her proud and aristocratic boss, she realised, but a sexually aroused stranger she didn't really recognise.

She pulled her sweater down over her aching breasts. 'What...what do you think you're doing?' she stumbled.

With an effort he sucked air back into his lungs and an unbearable frustration coated his words with bitterness. 'Oh, come on—Ashley. A little less of the outraged innocence,' he bit out. 'That kiss has been weeks in the making—you know that and I know that. And please don't pretend you didn't want it as much as I did. It's bad enough to be thwarted in a situation like this—but hypocrisy would make it simply intolerable.'

Shame washed over her. Ashley opened her mouth to protest—to fling his unjust accusations back at him—but how could she do that, when deep down she knew that he spoke nothing but the truth? This *had* been weeks in the making—if she was honest enough to admit to all the little glances and side-glances they'd exchanged. That feeling of excitement and frustration whenever he was around. And she couldn't deny that she *had* wanted it—maybe she was just taken aback by how much he seemed to want her, too...

She was confused and bewildered, and Ashley's instinct to escape overrode everything. Her cheeks burning with shame, she turned her back on him and ran—her footsteps slipping and sliding in the soft mud as she gathered pace.

'Ashley!'

She heard his angry roar from behind her but she

paid it no attention and carried on running, her breath coming in hot, painful gasps as she fled towards the house.

Once inside, she pulled off her muddy shoes and rushed upstairs to her room, staring at herself in the mirror in disbelief as she saw her unbuttoned coat and the rumpled sweater and remembered Jack's hand straying inside it and touching her there.

Briefly, she closed her eyes and swallowed as she recalled that brief burst of pleasure as his fingers had closed over her breast. And that disbelieving sense of joy as he had kissed her so passionately.

Yet the image in the mirror mocked her with its flushed cheeks and the normally neat hair tumbling down around her face. And if that kiss had made Jack into someone she didn't really recognise—couldn't the same be said about her? Was that wide-eyed creature really her?

Her thoughts spinning, she tried to put it into perspective. She was wary of men, yes—but she wasn't a prude. She knew that sex was part of life and long ago she had decided that she was going to hold out for love, if such a thing existed. She'd seen too many people sell themselves short—and the truth was that she'd never felt even a flicker of interest in a man before. Not before Jack. And then suddenly along had come this great big flame of desire which now threatened to engulf her.

But it was wrong on so many levels. Jack was her boss and he was an aristocrat. And things like that mattered. Rich and eligible landowners didn't form serious relationships with teenage girls who'd spent their life in the care system. Not unless they had traffic-stopping good looks and legs up to their armpits. They might want to take them to *bed*—to have a bit of a fling with them—but that was as far as it went. This was her *job* she was putting into jeopardy—a job she needed far too much to risk losing.

But you liked it, didn't you? You liked it a lot. For all your supposed high moral stance about men—you capitulated pretty quickly. Maybe you're more like your mother than you thought you were.

Her fingers shaking, she pinned her hair back and shook her head at her own flushed reflection. No! She was nothing *like* her mother.

And then to her horror she heard a knock on the door and knew it could only be one person.

'Ashley?'

She heard the dark note underpinning his voice and froze.

'Ashley, answer me! I know you're in there. Are you going to open the damned door?'

Her heart thundering, she stared at the dark oak barrier which lay between them. 'And if I don't?'

'Then you'll make me very angry indeed.'

Angrier than he already sounded? she wondered. But what choice did she have other than to open it? She could hardly barricade herself in there like some sort of cowering princess in a tower. She was going to have to come out and face him *some* time. Cautiously, she pulled open the door to find him standing there, his black eyes spitting out a series of conflicting messages. Anger, yes—and irritation, certainly. But she wasn't a fool—and only a fool would have denied the desire which still smouldered at their smoky depths.

He studied her. 'So why the dramatics? Why the hell did you run off like that?'

'Isn't it obvious?'

'Not really, no. Was it such a terrible thing which happened, Ashley? Do I repulse you so much that it made your flesh crawl?'

She blushed as she stared down at the ground—unwilling to meet the accusation in his eyes, terrified that he would see the naked longing in hers. 'You know you don't,' she answered quietly.

'Yes, I do know.' Frustration heated his blood, swamping all the guilt which coursed through his veins. And it took every ounce of self-possession he knew not to take her into his arms and kiss away that pious expression on her face. 'So what made you run away like that?' he questioned again. 'Were you afraid that I was going to have my wicked way with you out there on the hilltop, whether you liked it or not?'

Steadily, she lifted her eyes. 'It was wrong, Jack. You know it was wrong. We both do.'

Jack shook his head. How dared she—*she*—tell him what was right and what was wrong? Yet the irony was that she was speaking the truth—it *was* wrong—though she didn't have a clue why. And maybe he should listen to her. Turn his back and walk away while he still could—before he did something he might regret and brought a whole pile of repercussions crashing down around him. Instinct told him to go while he still could and that instinct was strong—but the siren call of his body was even stronger… 'Why was it wrong?' he demanded.

'Because…because I work for you. Because of who I am and who *you* are. We're worlds apart. Or rather, I don't come from your sort of world.' Her voice quietened. 'But you're an intelligent man, Jack—and you certainly don't need me to spell it out for you.'

His lips curved. 'So you're inhibited by old-fashioned ideas about social status, is that it? About your place in society and mine? Why, I'm disappointed in you, Ashley.'

'Well, don't be—it's the truth, and you know it.'

'Is it? Even if it was—I wasn't proposing we spend a lifetime together,' he added cuttingly. 'I just thought we could enjoy something which we have both been wanting for some time.'

It was the best thing he could have said—even if it was also the most hurtful. Because it reinforced what Ashley already suspected. That to Jack, she was just a commodity. Like a bottle of wine or a new shirt— she was something which he would use, enjoy and then ultimately discard. And where would that leave her? Creeping away from here shamefaced when the job ended—with him probably feeling disgusted at himself, maybe even giving her a lukewarm reference as a consequence, and jeopardising future job prospects into the bargain.

'Do you know why they say you should never mix

business and pleasure?' she returned hotly, his arrogance giving her the strength to fight her corner. 'Because it happens to be true.' She drew a deep breath as she struggled to convince herself. 'And it mustn't happen again, Jack. It mustn't. Do you understand?'

There was silence for a moment as he saw the determination written on her now-pale features and the exquisite irony of the situation didn't escape him. Quiet little Ashley Jones who had been on fire in his arms was now primly telling him that it was a no-go. Did she think he was going to fight to change her mind? Sweep her into his arms and make her rethink? Well, in that case—she was going to be very disappointed.

His mouth tightened. 'Very well, Ashley,' he said, his voice low. 'If that's what you want, then that's exactly what you'll get.' And, with a finality which took her breath away, he turned swiftly on his heel and walked away, leaving her staring at his retreating back as tears began to well in her eyes. Hotly, they pricked at her eyes as she sank down on the bed, burying her face in her hands and wondering how she could have let him go like that. Turned away the only man she had ever really wanted.

Because it was the right thing to do. The only thing to do. And if she was going to carry on working for him—then they had both better forget that it had ever happened.

It took a strange kind of courage to go and face him again, but Jack wasn't in the study when she went downstairs. In fact, there was no sign of him anywhere in the house—only a rather disconsolate-looking Casey sniffing around the place and looking as lost as he always did when his master wasn't around. And when Christine arrived later that day, carrying a whole load of shopping and provisions, unusually, she didn't ask where Jack was.

It was only when Ashley mentioned his name in a studiedly casual way that she received yet another shock.

'Have you spoken to Mr Marchant?' she asked the housekeeper.

Christine nodded as she slid a carton of orange juice into the fridge. 'Yes, he rang me just before he went off to London,' she answered.

Ashley's heart missed a beat. 'To London?' she repeated—some stupid element of hurt pride not wanting to admit that she didn't have a clue what the older woman was talking about.

'Didn't he tell you? No? Actually, I wondered when he'd be going down there again,' confided Christine. 'He hasn't been for ages, which is very unusual—not since you started working here, come to think of it.'

With an effort, Ashley kept her face blank. Even more hurtful than the thought that he hadn't bothered to tell her he was going was the realisation that Jack had a whole different life about which she knew precisely nothing.

But of course he did! What did she expect? That he should be languishing here, isolated from the world, just waiting for someone like her to walk into his life?

He had money, connections and a faintly glamorous profession, which he didn't even need to do because he was independently rich through his inheritance. Of *course* he had another life!

She tried to concentrate on his novel, which had now reached a nail-biting section involving some undercover work which was leading up towards a bloody ambush. But the work which she'd previously found so engrossing had lost something of its appeal and it wouldn't take a genius to work out why.

She missed the dark force of Jack's character as he sat working on the other side of the room. She missed the conversations they would have over their morning coffee. The way he would sometimes look up and the light from his dark eyes would pierce through her like a laser beam. And she missed feeling singled out by him—as if he thought she was somehow *special*. Mealtimes were dull without him and she felt like an imposter—as if she had no legitimate reason to be there. And the house felt empty—as if it had lost its heart and soul.

With spare time on her hands, she began to wonder whether Jack had been right and whether she was the world's biggest hypocrite. Because she *had* wanted him to make love to her and yet had denied it—even to herself. She had responded to him with all the passion of a woman and then run away like a frightened little girl. Had she been so scared of her own feelings that she didn't dare risk it—or was she just guarding herself against the possibility of being hurt by him?

She missed him more than she had thought it was possible to miss anyone. And then one morning she had to dodge round one of the cleaners, who was polishing the oak floor in the hall, and when she walked into the kitchen Ashley saw Christine bustling around on a day when she wasn't supposed to be working.

'Hello! I didn't know you were coming in today,' Ashley said.

The housekeeper put down the cookery book she'd been poring over. 'No, I wasn't—but Mr Marchant's coming back for the weekend!'

Ashley's heart began to pound with excitement as she told herself that it didn't matter that he hadn't bothered mentioning it to *her*. The most important thing was that Jack was coming home. Back home—where he belonged. He'd be walking into the study every morning just as he used to—with those dark, clever eyes watching her. Once more, they would spend long days together.

And if he tried to kiss her again—would it really be the end of the world? What if she just went with the flow and let him make love to her—as most women in her position would have done? Would that be so very wrong, given the feelings she had for him? Maybe it was time to stop acting like a little girl and to embrace all that went with being a woman. Ashley found herself grinning like an idiot as suitable words to express her joy seemed grossly inappropriate. 'That's…nice,' she managed.

'Is it?' Christine's tone was disapproving as she reached into the cupboard for some eggs. 'Not when he

suddenly announces he's bringing people with him—
and barely giving me enough time to do the catering.'

Ashley stilled as an unknown foreboding began
to creep over her skin. 'People?' she echoed quietly.
'W-what people?'

'Oh, some of his fancy friends, I expect.' The housekeeper gave a shrug. 'Those glamorous types who are
a *nightmare* to cook for—won't eat dairy, won't eat
wheat—never heard anything like it! That Nicole will
probably be among them. She usually is.'

Ashley's heartbeat now became dizzyingly erratic.
He was bringing people here? Well, of course he was.
What had she expected—that he might run it past *her*
first? 'Really?' she questioned, in a voice she didn't
quite recognise as her own.

'You would think,' continued Christine darkly, 'that
he would deal with his *other* commitments and priorities
at home, before he goes gallivanting off to London with
all those other women.'

But Ashley scarcely heard her. Vaguely, she wondered what the housekeeper meant by *commitments* and
priorities—but there were much more pressing issues
on her mind. *Those other women*, Christine had said.

What women? And who was 'Nicole'?

Bile rose in her throat. There she'd been—*like a
fool*—reading everything into that passionate kiss she'd
shared with Jack on the moor. Reading everything into
it when it had meant nothing to him. A sensual diver-
sion which must have given him a disappointing outcome. Why, he hadn't been in touch with her since—not

once—and he hadn't even bothered to tell her he was coming back.

And that he wouldn't be alone.

CHAPTER SIX

A CAR door slammed and Ashley's fingers stilled on the keyboard. She glanced up at the clock, surprised to see that it was after six. So Jack was home at last—bringing all his friends with him.

Outside, she heard doors slam, closely followed by footsteps, laughter—and throaty feminine giggles. So Christine had been right. A feeling of nausea rose in her throat but she sat as silently as a statue, praying she could stay undiscovered before slipping quietly upstairs when the coast was clear.

She stayed perfectly quiet until she heard the clip-clopping of high heels mounting the stairs. They were probably going to change for dinner, she thought—the elaborate dinner which Christine had been preparing for most of the afternoon.

And then the door opened and she felt her heart crashing against her ribs as Jack walked in. It was barely a week since she'd seen him and yet it felt as if a slow year might have passed. Dressed completely in black—close-fitting black jeans and a black cashmere sweater—his tall figure looked dark and imposing. His face was dark too and his expression unfathomable as he shut the door softly behind him.

Absence made him look startlingly unfamiliar and she tried to study his face objectively—as if it were the first time she'd ever seen it. There were shadows beneath his eyes, which made his expression look brittle, and she found herself thinking how tired he looked. She wanted to turn round and to slide her arms around his neck. She wanted him to kiss her.

'Hello, Ashley,' he said softly.

Ashley drew a deep breath. What would a secretary say to her boss if he *hadn't* kissed her? 'Jack! Hello. Nice to see you!'

There was a pause and, briefly, his eyes narrowed. 'You're working very late tonight.'

'Oh, it's only just gone six and I thought I'd crack on with it,' she said cheerfully. 'There's a lot which needs to be done—you made masses of changes in the middle section, the bit where they ambush the enemy camp.'

'How very diligent you are,' he observed drily.

'That's what you pay me for, remember?'

'Yes. Of course.' Another pause. 'I'd quite forgotten.'

Ashley hid her hurt behind an impassive smile even though she could feel the tell-tale steal of colour into her cheeks. Now she wanted to be anywhere but here—a million miles from that searching black stare. But she had to show him she didn't care. That she had put their stolen kiss behind her and she wasn't going to refer to it ever again. Their boss and employee relationship was back to where it should have been all along—on a purely professional footing. He had come close to seducing her that day on the moors, and she had had a lucky escape— because it seemed that there were other women all ready and willing to take her place. She would just never give him the satisfaction of knowing how much he had hurt her.

'Did you have a good time in London?' she questioned politely.

He made an impatient little sound beneath his breath as all his pent-up desire for her began to spiral up, astonished to find that his hunger for her hadn't abated— despite his determination that it should. Despite the fact that she had pushed him away and that deep down he kept telling himself that it had been the best possible outcome for everyone… But knowing that did nothing to quieten the insistent thudding of his heart—or the sudden jerk of lust at his groin. His gaze swept over her face, taking in the unadorned eyelashes and the bare lips. 'You look pale.'

'I do?'

'Very pale. Pale as chalk. Are you…okay?'

It was a veiled question and she quietened down the terrible urge to flare at him. To tell him that no, *of course she wasn't okay*. He had walked away from her as if she meant nothing and then replaced her with those giggling women she'd just heard arriving. But jealousy had no valid place in her life—even if their relationship *had* merited such feelings. Jealousy only ever harmed the person who expressed it. There was absolutely no point feeling jealous about a man like Jack. He operated in a different world—a different *universe*. Resolutely, she shook her head. 'No. Nothing's wrong.'

'No?' He put his head to one side and regarded her—a sudden mischief playing in his eyes. 'Did you miss me?'

Ashley bit her lip. That was so unfair. The question was as inappropriate as it was provocative and surely it was designed to embarrass both of them. Swallowing down the sadness and regret which had risen in her throat, she prayed her expression wouldn't give the game away. But what could she say other than a variation of the truth when Jack was perceptive enough to read an outright lie in her eyes? And she'd look an even bigger fool if he thought she was sulking about what had happened. 'The house was very quiet without you,' she said truthfully.

'Not a commendation I've ever been given before,' he commented. 'So is that a yes, or a no?'

'Maybe it's a mixture of both.'

'Oh, Ashley—how brutally you wound with your distinctive brand of honesty.' He gave a brief smile before his gaze flicked over the desk and looked at the neat pages of typescript. 'Leave that now. It'll be time for dinner soon.'

'But you've brought...*friends* with you, I understand?'

'Christine's been gossiping again, I suppose—or was it one of the cleaners?'

'Actually, I heard you all arriving.'

'Of course you did.' Thoughtfully, he noted the dejected slump of her shoulders. 'You'll join us, of course.'

'No, really. I couldn't. I'll—'

'You'll what?' he interrupted mockingly. 'Eat a sandwich in the solitude of your room? Or creep into the kitchen and consume the leftovers while we're drinking our coffee by the fireside?'

Did this mean she was to be brought out as an example of provincial entertainment to amuse his sophisticated London friends? she wondered. Or was he extracting some cruel form of punishment because she'd turned him down the other day? Silently, her eyes pleaded with him not to continue—but his expression didn't alter.

'We'll see you down here at eight,' he said.

'Is that an order?'

'Yes, it's an order.' His black eyes met hers. 'You respond very well to direction, I've found.'

'And what if I told you that I'm not very hungry?'

'I'd say it was irrelevant. Since when did hunger ever really play a part at dinner parties? I want you there—so go and get changed, Ashley, and I'll see you later.'

And with this, he strode from the study, leaving Ashley feeling flustered and slightly rebellious. Could she get out of going? For a moment she was tempted—until she realised she had no choice other than to fall in with his plans. A refusal to attend might look like defiance and somehow she knew that he wouldn't let her get away with it. She could easily imagine him storming up to her room and haranguing her until she complied with his wishes. Reluctantly, she went upstairs to shower and when she came out of the bathroom she could hear squeals of female laughter coming from the floor below.

Surveying the meagre contents of her wardrobe, she gave a grimace. She didn't own the kind of clothes which were suitable for a fancy dinner in a millionaire home and she pulled out the only dress which was halfway presentable. It was her 'best' dress and she'd chosen it mainly because it was so quiet and unmemorable that she could wear it lots of times without people realising they'd seen it before.

In soft grey silk, it skimmed her body rather than clinging to it, and she wore it with a single rope of fake pearls. As always, she scooped her hair off her face, but she left the style slightly softer than usual. Because while Jack might have gone out of his way to remind her that she was a member of staff, she didn't want to look as if she were about to start taking dictation!

Rarely had she felt so stricken with nerves as she went downstairs towards the sound of animated chatter. She kept telling herself that she had faced far worse in her life than a smart dinner party full of strangers. What about all the times she'd been sent to new foster parents—before becoming painfully aware that they were taking her in solely to earn themselves some extra money? And what about the times she'd seen disappointment on the faces of her newest 'family'—when they realised that the mousey little orphan they'd been allotted was lacking in any attractive characteristics?

'Ah, Ashley. Here you are.' Jack looked up as she walked into the room and his eyes narrowed—leaving her wondering if her choice of outfit was an appalling one.

Judging by those worn by the other two women, it might well be because she felt like some mediocre shadow in comparison. A statuesque brunette was shimmering in a thigh-skimming scarlet silk dress which complemented her long nails, while a cool blonde wore a shade of blue which perfectly matched her eyes. There was only one other person present—an elegant man with dark russet hair and an expression of mischief on his face. The three of them looked up and smiled at Ashley, and she did her best to smile back.

Jack stepped towards her and propelled her forward, his hand resting briefly at the small of her back—as if he was afraid that she might simply turn tail and run away again. And Ashley couldn't prevent her shiver of recognition as she felt him touch her. Did he remember the way they had kissed the other day, she wondered—or was kissing a woman no big deal to a man like him?

His brilliant black eyes gleamed down at her. 'Ashley—let me introduce you to everyone. This is Kate.'

'Hi, Ashley,' said the blonde, in a soft, Scottish accent.

'And this is…' he paused as the knockout brunette glanced up at him and smiled '…Nicole.'

At this, Nicole's smile became warmer. 'Hello, Ashley—Jack's told us all about you.'

'He has?'

'He certainly has. Says you're the only secretary who's never grumbled about his handwriting.'

'That's because I promised her a bonus if she didn't,' said Jack, and they all laughed.

But Ashley's smile felt forced—even though she prayed it didn't look that way. *Why* had he insisted she make an appearance? Things were bound to be difficult after what had happened between them and surely this would only make them worse. Didn't he realise that she felt out of place among his rich and elegant friends—no matter how friendly they seemed? And it didn't help that he looked absolutely amazing in a black dinner suit which seemed designed to emphasise the broad shoulders and long legs.

She wished that she could wave a magic wand and find herself somewhere else—but what choice did she have other than to stick it out with good grace? Dazzled by the circlet of emeralds strung around Nicole's slender neck, she realised that leaving now would do her no good except to make her look like an idiot instead of just *feeling* like one. She was going to have to endure this meal no matter how uncomfortable it might be—and she was going to have to do so with a certain amount of dignity. She turned to the russet-haired man with the mischief in his eyes and gave him a polite smile.

'I'm sorry,' she said quietly. 'I don't think Jack mentioned your name.'

The man laughed. 'Then he should have his knuckles rapped for a lack of etiquette, shouldn't he? My name's Barry Connally and I'm delighted to meet you. You deserve a medal for working for someone as irascible as this brute—but in the absence of a medal, you'd better have a glass of champagne instead.'

'No, thank you—honestly, I'm fine.'

'Ashley doesn't drink much alcohol. And anyway—' Jack's black eyes captured hers from across the room. '—I think dinner's ready—so why don't we go in?'

It felt strange for Ashley to troop into the dining room where she'd shared so many meals with her boss, when it had been just the two of them. Back then she'd found the setting rather formal until she had become used to it—but she'd never seen the room as dressed-up as it was tonight. Now *this* was formality, she thought, blinking a little as she looked around.

Christine and her team had certainly been busy because the table was laden with crystal, silver and crisp white linen which Ashley had never seen before. Tall, creamy candles flickered over bowls of white hyacinth which filled the air with their heavy scent. Rows of different knives and forks were lined up on either side of each place setting and she wondered just how many courses they were supposed to be eating. Would she know which implement to use, she wondered—or would she disgrace herself by eating with the wrong ones?

For Ashley, the meal felt a bit like an endurance test. It was strange to be sitting there, served by some young girls who had been shipped in from the village for the evening. She spent much of the meal in silence, listening to Barry Connally, who thankfully held forth with a constant stream of jokes.

But although Ashley was listening well enough to smile politely at each punchline, her attention was drawn to the interaction between Jack and the stunning brunette. Unwillingly, she watched as Nicole smiled up at him. How she giggled at pretty much everything he said. And how the glittering green of the emerald circlet at her neck drew attention to a magnificent cleavage, which tapered down to tiny waist. It might have been easier to bear if she'd been a bitchy kind of woman— but she wasn't. In fact, she went out of her way to chat to Ashley with a manner which wasn't in the least bit condescending. How could Jack fail to be mesmerised by such a woman?

After dessert, they all went into the library for coffee, where a fire roared in the grate and a tray of brandies and liqueurs had been placed on a side-table. It should have been a warm and welcoming scene but to Ashley it felt anything but—something she put down to the cold ache in her heart. Unnoticed, she crept over to the window and shrank down into a chair by the curtains, wondering how quickly she could make her escape— when Jack walked across the room and sat down beside her.

Up close, he looked even more magnificent, his aristocratic features seeming to have been hewn from marble and his raven hair gleaming blue-black in the firelight.

'You're very quiet tonight,' he observed.

'Am I?' She gave a little shrug. 'Everyone else is so bright and chatty that I hardly think my silence will be noticed.'

He raised his eyebrows. 'Do you make a habit of always putting yourself down, Ashley?'

'I prefer to think of it as being realistic.'

'Do you?' There was a pause as he studied her. Why was she being so damned *unresponsive*—as if the woman he had held in his arms on the windswept moor had been replaced with a waxwork replica? 'You know, you didn't give me a very satisfactory answer when I asked you a question earlier.'

'And which particular question was that, Jack?'

He gave a low laugh. 'When I asked whether you'd missed me.'

Quickly, Ashley glanced across the room—where Barry was in the process of pouring liqueurs for the two women. 'Do you want our conversation overheard by the whole room?' she whispered. 'Don't you think it might make them wonder why you're asking your secretary a question like that?'

'That's extremely unlikely to happen,' he drawled. 'Unless you're planning to break the habit of a lifetime by raising that soft voice of yours.'

'Whether I missed you or not is irrelevant,' she managed, her voice sounding little, and lost.

'Is it?' A smile touched the edges of his lips as he leaned forward. 'So what's the matter, Ashley? Your lips are trembling as if you're cold, yet the fire is blazing and the room is warm.'

You're making me want you and it is wrong to want you. We both know that. 'You're…you're neglecting your guests,' she whispered.

His laugh was as soft as it had been before, but now it was tinged with something else, something dangerous, which made the little hairs on the back of her neck prickle with a sense of the unknown.

'There goes that hypocrisy again,' he taunted. 'Your eyes are saying something which your lips are contradicting. You look like a hungry bird which has escaped the winter chill and hopped onto the window sill to find a whole heap of crumbs waiting there—and yet something stops you from reaching out to take them. You wanted me that day on the moor—but then you clammed up and pretended that you didn't.' His eyes gleamed. 'I don't really need a lesson in etiquette from you, Ashley, but perhaps you're right—I *am* neglecting them. So you'd better excuse me and I'll get back to them and leave you alone in your little ivory tower over here.'

With that, he stood up and went back to the others—leaving Ashley feeling even more isolated than ever and yet knowing she had only herself to blame. Her head was whirling from the bizarre conversation they'd just shared and all she wanted to do was to escape. *Was* she a hypocrite? she asked herself distractedly. Was that how she came across—as some kind of tease who liked to play games? Didn't he realise that she had simply been trying to protect herself and to maintain an air of professionalism between them? Yet now it seemed as though she had wrecked even that—wouldn't the worst of all possible scenarios be that she lost her job without ever having known what it was like to have Jack make love to her?

Quietly, she rose to her feet—though she noticed that Jack barely lifted his head to say goodnight as she excused herself and slipped from the room.

Once she was safely back in her bedroom, she undressed—but she noticed that her hands were shaking. And so was her body. Shivering violently, she climbed into bed, curling herself into a ball in a desperate attempt to warm herself, but inside she felt like a cold block of ice. From downstairs she could hear the distant strains of laughter and she pulled a pillow over her head to try to block out the sounds of the others as they made their way up to bed. But when the house had grown quiet, she found herself listening in the darkness—like a small animal who had found itself in an unknown and threatening place with no idea how to escape.

Pricking up her ears, she heard footsteps treading the night-time corridor. Yet these were not the distracted footsteps of Jack in one of his sleepless moods, but much lighter ones—though with a definite sense of purpose. Somewhere a door opened and closed again—and Ashley bit down hard on her lip as if doing that might alleviate the sudden clench of pain in her heart.

Was that the sound of Nicole creeping into Jack's bedroom? she wondered. Was she drawing back the duvet and slipping into bed beside him—his hard, naked body enfolding her to him? Behind Ashley's closed eyes the graphic images continued to dance—yet what right did she have to feel bitter, or resentful?

You had your chance! You had your chance with him—and you blew it. You threw it away.

But even knowing that it had been the right thing to do did little to soothe her troubled spirit. It had been a long time since Ashley had cried. There was absolutely no comparison to the night she'd been locked up by her cruel foster mother and lain in the cupboard there, trembling in terror. Yet somehow the thought of what she had almost found with Jack and had now seen snatched away was enough to make her heart clench. Silently, she turned her head and bit her lip, but that did nothing to stem the silent flow of tears.

CHAPTER SEVEN

SOMEHOW Ashley got through the rest of the weekend. She hid behind a calm smile and a determination not to let her feelings show—but she had never felt more of an outsider. Like an unwilling spectator, she watched from the sidelines as Jack played host to his houseguests—and it seemed to her that the lovely Nicole had been born to live a life like this.

A horse was sent up from the village and each morning, sitting astride the now-recovered Nero, Jack took the lustrous brunette horse-riding with him. Ashley saw them as they returned to the house, walking companionably together across the lawns, their faces flushed with exercise and animated in conversation. *Nicole* wasn't scared of horses. *She* didn't jump and startle them and make a man end up lying in a ditch. Ashley hated the sharp pang of jealousy which shot through her—and she hated the way her eyes always seemed to be drawn to the two of them. She had to snap out of it and stop thinking about him in that way—because it was none of her business.

But to her surprise, there was no sign of any deepening relationship between her boss and Nicole. In fact, Jack seemed more and more uninterested in the brunette as the weekend progressed, leaving Ashley feeling bewildered. It should have appeased her but it did not. If he failed to respond to someone as lovely, rich and cultured as Nicole—then what hope was there for her?

She was both relieved and nervous when the three houseguests finally departed—wondering what it was going to be like to be alone with him again. Safe in the confines of the office, she could hear the sound of laughter as they all said their goodbyes, but she blocked out the sounds and tried to concentrate on the manuscript.

When at last he came into the study she paused for a moment, letting her flying fingers still on the keyboard as he entered the room, her gaze drawn unwillingly to his face. His dark eyes were unfathomable as they looked at her and his face was faintly flushed.

'Good morning, Ashley,' he said softly.

She swallowed. 'Good morning.'

'The guests have gone.'

She nodded. 'So I heard.'

'Yet you didn't bother coming outside to wave them goodbye?'

'I had work to be getting on with. Anyway, I didn't really think it was my place to do that.'

'You didn't think it was your *place*?' he echoed in disbelief.

She paused, because the black eyes were now looking at her with a kind of impatience—as if he was waiting for an explanation. And maybe she should give him one. 'They're not my friends—they're yours.'

'Yes. So they are.' Slowly, he walked across the room and came to stand beside her. 'And what did you think of them?'

Why was he doing that—standing so close that she could barely breathe? From here she could make out the musky scent of soap and sandalwood as well as being aware of the sound of his breathing and the warmth of his body. Was he trying to tantalise her with his proximity—to remind her just how warm and vital he could be? With fingers which were threatening to tremble, Ashley put her hands in her lap where he couldn't see them. 'Surely my opinion on your friends is irrelevant.'

'Maybe it is—but I'm very interested to hear what you think. Your judgement always interests me,' he persisted. 'Or perhaps you're prevaricating? What's the matter, Ashley—don't you like my friends and are afraid to tell me?'

'I shouldn't dream of being so rude and neither would I dream of pronouncing judgement on them. But if you insist on having my opinion, then I'll give you one. I thought Barry was very funny.'

'Oh, he is.' His black eyes became momentarily flinty. 'Women are always captivated by his charm—though men can usually see right through it. And Nicole? What did you think of Nicole?'

'She...' Ashley sucked in a breath. 'She's very beautiful.'

'Yes, she is.'

And even though she hadn't seen any outward displays of affection, some masochistic urge made Ashley press on. 'She seems very…fond of you.'

Black eyes glittered. 'Can you blame her?'

'"Blame" isn't a word I usually associate with the giving of affection, Jack.'

'Oh, Ashley,' he said, his laugh soft and low. 'Can a man ever win an argument against you?'

'I wasn't aware that we were arguing.'

'Weren't you? Then I can only conclude that either you're extremely naïve or extremely disingenuous.' His features hardened as his gaze scanned her face like a searchlight, his lips curving into a smile. 'We often disagree. It's because we're deeply attracted to one another—and arguing is just one way of sublimating those feelings. The conflict we create on the surface is merely a foil to hide the desire which simmers beneath the surface. It's always there, Ashley. Always there.' His eyes gleamed. 'Can't you feel it? It's simmering now—hot and fierce and relentless. It's making me want to take you into my arms again just the way I did on the hill, when I kissed you and you responded with a passion which blew me away.'

'Jack—'

'I thought that a break might make me come to my senses. Might make me realise the folly of what nearly happened. I thought if I provided myself with social diversions, that I could dismiss the incident as irrelevant. I thought that perhaps I might make myself interested in Nicole—or Kate.' His eyes were gleaming now. 'But

I can't,' he said simply. 'It's you I want. I still want you.
I can't get you out of my mind, Ashley—and that's the
truth of it.'

'Jack,' she whispered again and the word sounded
breathless as it caught in her dry throat. He had just
said words she had never thought she'd hear—words
she had longed for in the dark and sleepless hours of the
night. But some bone-deep instinct told her that this was
wrong—and Ashley had spent too much of her life reli-
ant on what her instincts were telling her to ignore them
now. She shook her head. 'Please, Jack,' she finished.

'Please what?' he questioned, his voice hardening
into a husky taunt.

She swallowed down her own desire. 'Stop talking
that way.'

'What way is that?'

'We *mustn't*!'

'Stop telling it like it is, you mean?' he forged on, as
if she hadn't spoken.

She shook her head, wanting this warm cloud of dangerous desire to evaporate.

'You're denying that it exists—this feeling between
us?' he challenged. 'In which case perhaps my honest
Ashley is telling a lie for once.'

Once more, she shook her head—yet she couldn't
deny his words. There *was* desire. Deep and strong and
all-consuming. She could feel it right now—making
itself known to a body which had no practice in resis-
tance techniques. All she knew was that her mouth had
dried and she wanted him to kiss her again. She wanted

to feel the hot crush of his lips and the powerful strength of his body as he pulled her into his arms. Swallowing convulsively like someone who had a fishbone stuck in their throat, she stared up at his half-parted lips. 'It isn't…appropriate,' she breathed.

'Appropriate?' he echoed and something in his voice made Ashley start.

She was so used to seeing the autocratic set of his proud features that sometimes it was difficult to imagine that he'd led others into battle. He had seen what most people would never see in a lifetime, nor wish to. But she caught a glimpse of that man now. War was elemental but so was sex—and she saw a flash of raw emotion tighten his features. It was difficult to say what that emotion was: a curious hybrid of anger, desire and something else—something which kept Ashley frozen to the spot until, without any kind of warning, he pulled her up from the chair and into his arms. His breath was warm against her face and she could feel his powerful hands imprisoning her waist.

'Why are you such a meek little mouse, Ashley?' he bit out, his eyes blazing black fire over her skin. 'Who cares what is "appropriate"? For once in your life—don't you long to reach out and take what you really want instead of standing on the sidelines and letting it pass you by?'

She didn't know whether he was expecting an answer and even if she'd been in any kind of coherent state to give him one she doubted words would have been able to pass her lips. As it was, she just stared up into the shifting shadows of his features, knowing what he was about to do and powerless to stop him. Uncertainly, her lips parted as he moved closer. For a moment he just stared down into her face, his black eyes almost unseeing. Until, with a small moan, he drove his mouth down on hers.

It was powerful and it was all consuming—a hot melding of the flesh, which started an instant fire of response singing in her blood. Her arms reached up for him and she clung to him. Into the warm cavern of her mouth, she heard him groan her name and she felt her body shiver in response.

'Ashley,' he groaned.

'Jack!' she cried brokenly, unable to contain her pent-up emotions any longer.

Tangling his fingers in her hair, he deepened the kiss as desire shot through her. Beneath that sweet onslaught she began to tremble uncontrollably and he must have felt it because he drew his mouth away—reached out his finger to trace it down her cheek until it stopped on her trembling lips.

'I want you,' he stated unequivocally.

She could taste his finger on the tip of her tongue. 'J-Jack.'

'And you want me,' he continued unsteadily. 'Don't you?'

How could she deny it any longer? How could she resist her heart's desire. 'Yes.' Yet even as she whispered her assent she felt insecurity begin to bubble up inside her—because she could not bear unasked questions to come back to haunt her. 'But what about…?'

As her words tailed off his eyes narrowed. 'About what?'

'Nicole.' She swallowed. 'Isn't she more suitable? More your type. Someone who rides horses. Someone who—'

'Shh.' He silenced her by placing a finger over her lips. 'I don't want to talk about Nicole. I want *you*, Ashley. I have wanted you from the moment I first set eyes on you. It's inexplicable and yet it's all powerful. You're like a fire that burns in my veins—do you know that? A fever I can't escape. Your quietness and your stillness have invaded my soul and I must have you. I must.'

It was a powerful declaration which made Ashley tremble again—even though she feared that this was wrong on so many levels. But hot on the heels of common sense came the growing realisation that her own desire matched his—despite the disparity of their age and experience. She could see her own hunger reflected back from his ebony eyes. She could feel every fibre of his body straining as if it were being pulled irresistibly against hers. And wasn't her own body doing exactly the same? Weren't they acting like two *magnets*? Each drawn inexplicably to the other?

'Jack,' she whispered, and let her head sink against his shoulder.

'Oh, Ashley. Don't you know what you do to me when you say "Jack" like that?' he demanded. 'You make me want to carry you upstairs and undress you—to reveal the delights I can only imagine lie beneath the clothes you wear. To pull the pins from the hair you always hide so resolutely from my eyes and to see it tumble and spill over my pillow in rich and gleaming profusion.' He stopped, a pulse beating frantically at his temple, and when he spoke again his voice was lower and much more urgent. 'Yet for once you are strangely silent—and I wonder why. No protests about my bold declaration to make love to you? No tearing yourself from my arms and fleeing to your room like last time?'

The whole world hung on her answer. Ashley could hear a universal silence within the space of two heart-beats as unfamiliar emotions threatened to overwhelm her. She could feel the desire which heated her blood—the same desire which had driven men and women since the beginning of time. But along with that new and primitive need came something else—something much more complex.

Because she saw something of herself in Jack—even though he was rich and powerful and she was broke and relatively subservient. Something in his spirit spoke to hers. His hunger was her hunger—their needs perfectly matched. As if some mischievous destiny had decided to pair them off without caring about the consequences.

'No,' she answered quietly, lifting her head and meet-ing his questioning gaze. 'This time I will not run from you. I can't. Not any more. I couldn't bear to go through my life not having known what it was like to be your lover, Jack.'

His jaw clenched—as if her heartfelt words had touched him—and then he made a little growl of pleasure at the back of his throat. 'In that case, you'd better come right back here into my arms, right now,' he said unsteadily. 'Hadn't you?'

'Yes,' she whispered back.

He explored her face with his kisses. First her eyelids and then the tip of her nose. His lips grazed over her cheeks and along the curve of her jaw. His mouth tickled against the lobes of her ears until she began to shiver helplessly. His tender seduction melted her completely until suddenly he drew his lips away from hers.

'I could take you here,' he said unevenly. 'I could seduce you in a hundred places, but I think we'd better go upstairs, don't you?'

'Yes,' she whispered as he laced his fingers with hers—so for one brief moment she stupidly imagined them standing together at an altar.

But if you let him make love to you then you must banish all foolish thoughts of anything lasting, she told herself fiercely. *He might take you to his bed, but he'll never marry you.*

He led her out to the staircase, jerking his dark head towards its curved ascent—his dark eyes gleaming as they sent out a provocative challenge. 'You want me to carry you?'

She shook her head. She didn't want to feel like some humble secretary being led off towards her unwilling fate by her powerful boss. 'No, we'll walk up there together. I'm not helpless.'

No, indeed she was not, thought Jack. In fact, she confounded expectation. 'Most women would revel in the fantasy of being swept off to bed by their lover on their first time together,' he mused.

Something in his words sent warning bells ringing as they climbed the stairs with their fingers entwined. *Most women?* How many women would that be? she wondered—knowing that there was nothing she could do to protect herself against the possibility of heartbreak. Not now. Because never had her destiny seemed so clearly defined as in that moment.

But something of Ashley's nerve deserted her as she stared at what lay ahead of her.

The closed oak door which led to Jack Marchant's bedroom.

CHAPTER EIGHT

THE doors swung soundlessly open and Ashley's eyes widened as she stepped inside her boss's bedroom. Sumptuous and very traditional—it was every bit as impressive as she had imagined it might be and dominated by a dark and vast four-poster bed. Her heart missed a beat. Was she crazy—wanting to be made love to by a brooding aristocrat of Jack's calibre?

'Don't look so nervous,' he said softly.

'I…I didn't realise I was.'

'You look terrified.'

'Do I?'

He noticed she didn't deny it. Shutting the door behind them, he took both her hands in his, turned them over and studied them—as if he was reading both her palms. And then he lifted his eyes to hers. 'And you're cold,' he observed.

Ashley nodded. 'A little.'

He drew her closer, so that she was cocooned in the warmth of his arms, and he dipped his lips to her ear. 'It may seem strange to undress you to make you warm again—but that's what I am about to do.'

She should have felt terrified by his assurance—by the trace of sensual confidence in his voice. But the truth was that when he was holding her like that—Ashley felt safe. Not some kind of inexperienced virgin who had been brought to the bed of an experienced man, but a woman who had met and found her match and was about to be initiated into the deep mysteries of love-making. 'Yes, please,' she whispered.

Gently, he unbuttoned her cardigan—sliding each button free in an act which somehow seemed to take on an erotic significance of its own. He slid down the side zip of her skirt so that it fell with a whisper to her ankles and some instinct told her to step out from within its confining circle. Her T-shirt was quickly disposed of until she stood in nothing but her bra and pants and a pair of dark tights. She should have felt shy—because surely he wasn't used to women who wore such plain and cheap underwear?

Yet Ashley felt no shyness, for wasn't this the most natural act in the world between a man and a woman—and wasn't she determined that he should see her for who she really was? Not a fantasy or a substitute or someone he could transform into something she wasn't, but a real person. Her. Ashley. Ashley Jones.

She stared at him from unblinking eyes. 'What should I do next?'

'You come here, my sweet little minx,' he said softly, entranced by her mixture of shyness and curiosity.

Stepping forward, she put her arms around his neck as she raised her lips to be kissed and momentarily she saw his face harden—as if something in that simple gesture had disturbed him. But the moment passed as soon as his lips brushed against hers and this time he *did* lift her up and carry her over to the vast bed, drawing back the feather-soft duvet before laying her down upon the mattress. She lay there, perfectly still—just staring up at him—scared to move or to do the wrong thing.

'Ashley,' he said sternly. 'Cover yourself up.'

Uncertainty crossed her face. 'Because you don't like what you see?'

He gave a short laugh. 'Are you kidding? Because I like it too much. But you'll get cold and you will distract me—come to think of it, you *are* distracting me.' His eyes glinted as he leaned over and pulled the duvet up to her chin—his eyes mock-stern. 'And a man who undresses before a woman for the first time shouldn't have trembling fingers.'

But as he peeled his dark sweater over his head Ashley thought he sounded bemused—as if his fingers weren't usually given to trembling.

She watched him undress—mesmerised as he gradually revealed his magnificent body to her rapt gaze. A silk shirt fluttered forgotten to the floor to lie beside his discarded jeans and a pair of boxers tumbled on top—until at last he stood there in all his naked magnificence. Every sinew and nerve fibre was drawn in delicious detail beneath the burnished surface of his dark skin and she was acutely aware of the dormant power in his large frame.

'You don't look away,' he observed softly as he came

across the room towards her. 'No shyness now, then, Ashley?'

Would it make her sound shameless if she admitted that there was none at all? That this seemed as natural to her as breathing—despite her inexperience? As if she was poised on the edge of a discovery—about to be initiated by the man whom she had grown to adore. In her mind, she tested out the word. Wasn't 'adore' too mild a description of her feelings for Jack? Didn't *love* fit the bill much better? She shook her head as her eyes drank in his unashamed arousal. 'No.'

'And no fear?'

She shook her head. 'No—definitely no fear.'

He gave a soft laugh as he joined her on the bed, pulling the soft cloud of the duvet over them, so that their bodies were warm and close beneath it. 'You are a constantly evolving series of revelations,' he murmured. 'Time after time you surprise me—this hardened sceptic who had never thought that he might be surprised by a woman again. I'm worried that you're suddenly going to come to your senses and wonder what the hell you are doing here in bed with me.' He began to pull the grips from her hair and stroked it as it fell freely onto the pillow. 'Mightn't you?'

She stared up into his face, touched the tips of her fingers against the hard rasp of his jaw and felt it graze them slightly. 'No, Jack,' she whispered as she moved to trace the softer flesh of his lower lip, and to linger there. She loved him, she realised—as she leaned her face a little closer. 'You won't get any doubts from me.

I've…I've never been more sure of anything in my life.'

'Oh, Ashley,' he remonstrated on a murmur. 'Didn't anyone ever teach you to hide what you really meant with layers of subterfuge? Don't you realise that's part and parcel of being a woman?'

She heard the unmistakable regret as he asked it, when surely regret had no place between them—not when they were doing something like this? Faint misgivings skittered over her skin—and maybe he noticed her brief frown because he leaned forward and brushed his lips over hers.

'Forgive me my cynicism,' he said in an odd voice. 'Do you think you can do that?'

She looked up at him and felt her heart swell with love and trust. 'Of course I can,' she whispered, reaching her hands up to his face. 'I think I can forgive you anything, Jack.'

For a moment a terrible tortured look crossed over his dark features—and she wondered what she'd said wrong—but the look was quickly replaced by desire. He bent his head and his sudden urgent kiss drove away all her questions and left nothing but a dreamy longing. She felt the longing build as he began to stroke her body, his practised touch making her move restlessly beneath his fingers.

'You're still wearing your bra,' he observed unevenly.

'So…so I am.'

'And your panties.'

'Yes.'

'I think we ought to do something about that, don't you?'

With one hand, he unclipped her bra and then slid her briefs down over her trembling thighs. 'You know that your skin,' he said unevenly as his lips brushed over the hollow at the base of her throat, 'is like purest silk.'

'Is it?'

'Mmm. If I could make a shirt from it, I'd never take it off.'

'Jack…'

'Mmm?' He kissed her until she was mindless with pleasure and stroked her until she thought she would go crazy. He seemed to want to take all the time in the world, coaxing and caressing her until she had reached melting point, when suddenly the mood changed. Drawing away from her, he looked down into her face, smoothing her tousled hair away from her flushed cheeks. 'I hate to break the mood,' he murmured, 'but there is something I need to do.'

She watched as he leaned across her and extracted a small foil packet from the bedside table and she knew that she had to tell him.

'Jack—' She saw his eyes narrow as he turned his head.

'For God's sake.' His voice was unsteady. 'If you want to change your mind, then you'd better tell me now!'

'No. I don't want to change my mind. I need…I need you to know something. You know that I'm…I'm a…'

'You're what, Ashley?' He pulled her back into his arms. 'A virgin, perhaps?' he supplied drily.

She swallowed. 'You knew?'

'Of course I knew.'

Did that mean that her lack of experience was making her a bad bed-partner? Had she been doing everything wrong? 'How can you tell?' she whispered.

'Oh, sweetheart—you couldn't be anything *but* a virgin—it's written in your every gesture. You respond with such a delicious combination of innocence and desire. But if…if you've suddenly decided that your innocence is too precious to squander on a hardened cynic like me—then you'd better tell me. If you want to go, then go. In fact, maybe for both our sakes it would be better if you did.' His voice roughened and a sombre note entered it. 'Only for God's sake do it quickly.'

She could see the huge effort it must have cost him to say that—just as she could feel the tension which was making his body so taut. Did he really think that she could just get up and walk away from here—when she had wanted him for so long? 'Of course I don't want to go. I want to stay here. With you.'

For a moment he seemed to struggle to contain himself—and then at last he gave a ragged sigh. 'You are beautiful,' he whispered, against the spill of her hair. 'Do you know that? Truly and properly beautiful. Inside and out.'

Yet strangely, the word jarred and Ashley felt a fleeting sense of disappointment as his body moved over hers. She wasn't 'beautiful' at all—*that* was a lie. So did it follow that everything else he'd said to her was untrue? But there was no time to question him—because a different kind of tension had now entered his body and something of that tension was beginning to flow into her.

Suddenly, she was on fire—every kiss dragging her deeper and deeper into the dark sensuality of this erotic new world. Jack's world. One where her senses were scrambled and every instinct in her body was crying out for something she didn't really understand.

But when he thrust into her, she was more than ready for him and the pain was so brief that she barely felt it. And didn't some darkly primitive emotion revel in the fact that it was Jack who had pierced her and given her that pain—and then replaced it with a pleasure so exquisite that his name was torn from her lips? Jack who had made her change from girl to woman.

'Jack,' she cried out as he pulled her down towards a dark, sweet vortex before tossing her out again, helpless on the tide. At first he was gentle with her, his movements slow and seeking as she relaxed into him. And then his movements became harder and faster, his kiss more hungry and intense. She felt like a piece of elastic which was being stretched and stretched—until at last it snapped and she cried out his name. And only when her back began its helpless arch did he begin to shudder within her, his arms tightening as he cradled her, his quickened breath fanning her bare shoulder until gradually he stilled. *I love him*, she thought fiercely as she clung to him, feeling the moist-satin of his sweat-sheened back.

After a few moments he let her go and rolled onto his back but, to Ashley's surprise, he didn't say a word. Thank heavens she hadn't blurted out how much she cared—because there was nothing coming back from him. In fact, the only thing that Jack had spoken of was desire. She risked a glance and could see him staring up at the ceiling as if he didn't really see it at all. In the silence of the room, she could sense his sudden disquiet.

Was he regretting what had just happened—and worrying that she would now read far too much into it? Perhaps this was a rite of passage for every woman who became his secretary. Perhaps the words he had spoken to her were the same he used to everyone. She felt a bitter lurch of pain in her heart as she wondered if he had a time-honoured method for removing them from his bed.

As she listened his breathing became steady, until its deep and regular rhythm told her that he had fallen asleep. And despite all her feelings of uncertainty and insecurity, Ashley felt glad. Because Jack needed to rest—and mightn't sleep dissolve some of the strain which always seemed to lurk around the corners of his eyes?

She stared up at the ceiling, feeling as disorientated as someone who found themselves in a strange city at the dead of night. Did she lie here until he was dead to the world so that she could make her escape? Surely that was preferable to having what was bound to be an extremely embarrassing conversation if she left it until he woke up. She swallowed. What would she say? Even worse, what would *he* say?

I'm sorry, Ashley—I don't know what came over me.

I'm sorry, Ashley—but you can no longer work for me.

Could she bear to look into his beloved face and see regret written there? And could she bear to witness the dark serpent of shame which would creep into their lives and sully what was left of their relationship? Gingerly, she began to slide away from him—until a hand closed like a vice around her naked waist and a slumberous deep voice shattered the silence.

'Where the hell do you think you're going?' he questioned softly.

CHAPTER NINE

JACK'S question cut into Ashley's confusion and as his eyelids slowly opened she found herself staring into the jet gleam of his brilliant eyes.

'I said, where are you going, Ashley?' he questioned softly. 'Creeping out of my bed without even a word goodbye? That isn't exactly a glowing recommendation of my love-making—and not particularly good for a man's ego, either.'

As if *he* needed anything to bolster his ego! 'Back…'

'Back?' he drawled. 'Back where?'

Say something reasonable, she urged herself. *Something which will give you time to work out how to feel comfortable around him after what has happened. And which will put his mind at ease that you aren't going to start coming over all needy.* Because needy didn't work. It made people push you away. She'd learnt that lesson as a frightened little four-year-old and she had never forgotten it. 'Back to the manuscript I'm supposed to be typing.'

'Really?' His eyes narrowed. 'Don't you think that's taking the work ethic a touch too far?'

'Not really. It's still only...' She glanced at the inexpensive little watch on her wrist, which was the only thing she was still wearing, and gave a little yelp of horror. 'Oh, my goodness—it's nearly four o'clock!'

'So what? I'm the boss and what I say goes,' he said, in a voice of soft mockery. 'We have as many hours as we want—and so many endless possibilities about how to spend them—and *you're* just itching to get back to your computer!'

'I'm only trying to be diligent,' she said.

'Sometimes a man doesn't want diligence.'

'No?' Her tongue snaked out to moisten her suddenly bone-dry lips because the way he was looking at her was making her feel boneless and melting. 'Not even from his secretary?'

'No. Not even from his secretary. Can't you think what he might prefer?'

'I'm...I'm not sure.'

'This.' He kissed her, stirring lazily as he brought her naked body to lie on top of him and her mouth hovering within kissing range. 'He prefers this.' Jack flicked his tongue over her lips. God, she tasted good. Sweet and wholesome and yet as sexy as any woman had a right to be. His hand reached down to find her honeyed moistness and he heard her little gasp of pleasure as she squirmed beneath his seeking fingers.

'Jack!'

'You are very responsive,' he murmured approvingly as he felt her writhe against his hand.

'Am…am I?' All she knew was that he seemed to set her on fire with every look and every touch and every kiss.

'Mmm.' Jack reached for a condom. She was eager and yet acquiescent as he parted her thighs and brought himself deep inside her—revelling in her hot and tight welcome as he began to move. And this time he watched her. This time he *saw* the pleasure which transformed her face into one of mindless rapture—before he too was caught up in its spell.

Afterwards she fell against him, nestling sleepily against his chest. 'That was…amazing,' she said shyly.

'No. *You* are amazing,' he said softly as he smoothed back the hair which was falling over her face. 'Though I confess it's a little strange to see my Ashley looking so wild and so uncontained.'

Her heart missed a beat as she opened her eyes. Did he mean it when he said 'my' Ashley like that or was it just a slip of the tongue—a careless statement said in the aftermath of making love?

'And an Ashley who is uncharacteristically silent,' he continued, tilting her chin a little—so that there was nowhere to look except at him. 'Are you having second thoughts about what just happened?'

'No.' She shook her head. 'Are you?'

He paused for a moment—and then an odd light entered his dark eyes. 'If I stopped to think about it long enough then I could find a whole list of reasons why it shouldn't have happened. But it's been building for weeks now. We both know that.' He trickled his finger from neck to breast. 'It was inevitable.'

He made it sound like a storm—a violent and un-expected storm which had now passed—and he hadn't exactly answered her question, had he? Ashley felt a tremor of foreboding. So was this to be the end of it—a one-off liaison which must now be forgotten?

'You realise that I know practically nothing about you,' he said suddenly.

Ashley swallowed. 'Perhaps...perhaps we should have had *that* conversation a couple of hours ago.'

'I'm serious, Ashley—don't be so evasive.'

Yet surely *he* was the one who had made evasion into an art form. Who clammed up whenever she tried to find out anything about his past and blocked any attempts to question him. But he was the boss and she supposed that gave him the right to ask questions—even in a set-ting like this one. 'What would you like to know?' she hedged. 'You've read my CV.'

'I'm not talking about your qualifications! I want to know more about you. I know your parents are dead but that's about all. What about brothers and sisters—do you have any?'

Awkwardly, Ashley shifted, wishing that she could just pull away from him and roll to the other side of the rumpled bed—away from the temptation of his body and the questions in his black eyes. Her past was a coun-try she had no wish to revisit and usually she fielded questions about it with a self-protective zeal and for good reason. People tended to judge you when you'd had an unconventional upbringing. But Jack was the man to whom she had just given her virginity—who had just made her feel things she'd never expected to feel. Wouldn't it be bizarre to withhold information from him when he was just trying to get to know her better?

'No, I don't. I'm an only child,' she said reluctantly. 'And my mother died when I was small.'

'What about your father?'

There was a pause while Ashley considered her options. Jack might seem interested in her past but when it boiled down to it—he was descended from a rich and well-connected family. Wouldn't he be appalled by the truth behind her circumstances? *But you can't hide it from him—for there should be no secrets between lovers. And wouldn't it be better if he knew everything from the outset—so that he can reject you sooner, rather than later?*

'I never knew my father.' She forced the words out. 'In fact, I don't know if my mother knew him either.'

'And what's that supposed to mean?'

Hadn't she always been honest with him? 'One of my foster mothers used to take great delight in telling me that my mother was a...a slut.' Ashley swallowed, her fingernails digging into the palms of her clenched hands. 'And that she slept with men in order to buy drugs.'

His eyes narrowed. 'Are you trying to shock me, Ashley?'

'No, I'm telling you the plain and unvarnished truth,

Jack—I thought that's what you wanted. How do I know whether or not it will shock you? You've seen more terrible things in your army days than most men would wish to see in a lifetime.'

He gave an odd kind of laugh as he thought how cleverly she had turned the question round and how, unwittingly, she had struck a blow at his conscience. 'Did someone once teach you the seductive power of truth?' he questioned, aware that he was skating on very thin ice indeed—but, ruthlessly, he closed his mind to it. Instead he pulled her closer and let her aroused and very feminine scent remove the thoughts which so troubled him.

She shook her head. 'I wasn't taught anything of any use.'

'Oh, yes, you were.' He took her by the shoulders, his fingers biting into her soft, bare flesh, and his black gaze burned into her. 'Somewhere along the way you learned how to burrow beneath a man's skin with quite stunning effectiveness.'

'Don't say these things to me, Jack,' she whispered.

'Don't you like compliments?'

'Only if they're true.'

'Oh, they're true, all right. Every word.' But he frowned as he heard the suspicion in her voice and thought about what she'd told him. 'It must have been a tough childhood,' he observed slowly.

She wondered what it would be like to admit to one of those 'normal' households, so beloved of advertisers. Mummy and Daddy and perhaps a sibling, or two.

The shiny car on the drive and the shared family meals around a table. Birthday cakes and Christmas trees and a pet dog who would chew their shoes and make them all laugh with careless indulgence.

And yet some instinct told Ashley that she wouldn't be lying here if she'd had that type of childhood. Because hadn't the hardship and loneliness she'd experienced—all the stuff which had damaged her—hadn't that forged some kind of strange bond between them? Because in ways she couldn't quite put her finger on, she recognised that Jack was damaged too. Was it just his experience in the army which had made him like that?

'It was difficult,' she said carefully.

'How difficult?'

She bit her lip as the memories came rushing in on a dark tide. 'Where do I begin? I mean, is there really any point in reliving the past and remembering all the foster parents who shouldn't have been let near a child? The ones who did it for money or to fill up the empty spaces in their own bad relationships? The ones who…' Her voice tailed off.

His face darkened. 'The ones who hit you?'

She shook her head. 'They didn't hit me.'

'Were cruel to you, then, in some other way?'

She remembered the locked cupboard and the sense of imprisonment. The walls closing in on her until she felt as if she couldn't breathe. The expression of shock on the doctor's face. The breath caught in her throat as she stared at him. 'How did you know that?' she whispered.

'Instinct, I guess. An instinct which can seek out suffering and can read pain.' And then he swore very softly. 'All your life you've been taken advantage of,' he added bitterly. 'And now I've just done exactly the same.'

She shook her head. 'But you haven't taken advantage of me, Jack! How could you have done when I wanted it, too? You know I did. There was no force—nor even any persuasion. We were two adults who wanted the same thing.'

'And you had no experience. None whatsoever. While I had plenty. Enough to know when to stop it. I should have taken control,' he said. 'I should have ended it while I still could.'

He's making excuses, Ashley realised—and she had to let him go if that was what he wanted. She mustn't chain him to her side because of a sense of guilt, or responsibility. 'It can end right now and right here. If you want it to.'

He stared down into her face for a long moment and then he laughed.

'Damn you, Ashley Jones,' he said softly as he pulled her back into his arms. 'Damn you for your soft understanding and your perception. Don't you know that by offering me freedom, you have guaranteed my willing capture?'

'That wasn't my intention.'

'You think I don't realise that? That you are totally without guile?' He gave a short laugh. 'I could put it down to your youth and inexperience—but it goes much deeper than that.' He stared deep into her eyes and lowered his voice to a murmur. 'You just have these instincts which make you remarkable and which make me hunger for you. I want you, Ashley, and I want you *now*.'

He pulled her against him and once more he began to make love to her—kissing her long and deep until she was more than ready for him once more. But his tenderness seemed to have been replaced by something else. She thought she sensed anger as he moved deep inside her—or could it have been *despair*? Afterwards, she must have fallen asleep because when she opened her eyes again the light had almost disappeared from the sky outside.

She blinked as she realised how late it must be. 'I really *am* going to have to do some work now, Jack.'

'You don't need my permission to get out of bed.'

'Well, I did last time I tried. Remember?'

Reluctantly, he laughed. 'So you did,' he murmured. 'Well, then, you'd better run along, before the memory of how you've just been wrapping those delectable thighs around my back makes me drag you back into my arms again.'

'Jack!'

'Don't you know I love it when you blush like that?'

'I am *definitely* getting up!'

'Go on, then. I'm not stopping you.'

He lay back against the bank of pillows as she rose from the rumpled sheets. She looked like a modern-day Venus, he thought contentedly—all tousled and rosy.

'Stop staring at me,' she whispered.

'But I like staring at you.'

For a moment, Ashley felt self-conscious as she made her way over his priceless silk rugs—wondering if he was judging her appearance. Wasn't that the kind of thing which all men did? Assessed naked bottoms and thighs on a scale of one to ten and decided whether or not they were wobbly? Scooping up her clothes, she carried them into his bathroom, where the image reflected back from the mirror stopped her in her tracks and she stared at it in disbelief.

Could that *really* be her? Mousey and unassuming Ashley Jones, her hair all loose and streaming down over her bare shoulders and her body all flushed and naked? Her fingers crept up to her mouth, which had been kissed so thoroughly by Jack that her lips were now the colour of crushed berries.

She washed and dressed, but when she walked back into the bedroom it was to discover that Jack had gone and the bed was empty. For a moment she just stood there, wondering if she had dreamt the whole thing— until the soft aching at the very core of her body reminded her that it had been very real.

So now what did she do? Go looking for him or just slide behind her desk and carry on working as if nothing had happened?

Walking over to the window, she stared at the darkening garden and then up at the sky, where the faint pinpricks of stars were beginning to sprinkle the skies. Was this how it was going to be from now on—her life inhibited by what had just happened? Not daring to express herself for fear of how it might be interpreted by her boss? No. She had to behave normally—if she could only remember how.

She was so lost in her thoughts that she didn't hear the door opening behind her—nor realise that anyone had entered the room until she heard the sound of something heavy being put down and then the soft whisper of lips at the back of her neck.

Turning around, she found Jack standing there—his rugged features flushed and his eyes gleaming dark.

'I wondered where you'd gone,' she whispered—wondering whatever had happened to all her good intentions about carrying on as normal. Did 'normal' include running her fingertips through the thick raven hair with a sense almost of wonder? Or leaning forward to inhale that raw masculine scent of soap and sandalwood which was all his—and dancing her lips in front of his.

'And did you miss me?' he murmured.

Once before he had asked her that same question and back then she had fudged the answer in order to protect herself from her growing feelings for him. But now—surely—there was no need to erect barriers, not when he had torn them down with the heady power of his love-making. Her finger brushed against his lips.

'Yes, I missed you. I missed you a lot,' she said. 'Where did you go?'

'I was getting us a drink.'

Looking over his shoulder, she could see a tray with

champagne and glasses sitting on a table. 'Champagne?' she questioned, on a note of surprise.

'I feel like champagne, don't you?' He walked over to the table and eased the cork from the bottle with a loud pop, before pouring two fizzing glassfuls and handing her one. 'Here.'

'Thanks.' Ashley took the glass and gave it a wistful smile. 'I've never drunk champagne in a man's bedroom before.'

'Then your education is only just beginning, Miss Jones,' came his mocking reply. 'But before we go any further—I think we'd better get something straight between us.' His voice was suddenly serious as his eyes captured hers. 'Nobody must find out about this, Ashley. Not Christine—not anybody. Do you understand? This is between you and me—nobody else.'

Ashley's smile didn't falter—though inside her heart was racing. Did that mean he was ashamed of her? Ashamed of his own weakness in having chosen her as his lover—rather than someone like Nicole who would have been a million times more suitable? But maybe he'd chosen his secretary because he could guarantee her obedience. Her willingness to please. And her reluctance to ask him why. Did he realise that her own insecurities meant that she wouldn't do anything which might threaten this precious bubble of happiness which was enveloping her?

'Of course I do,' she said.

'Good.'

But the champagne tasted sour on her lips and

did nothing to dull the urgent questions in her mind. Wouldn't any other woman who valued herself have objected to his desire for secrecy?

And didn't secrecy imply that there was something *wrong* about what they were doing?

CHAPTER TEN

'So what would you like to do this afternoon, my little green-eyed minx?'

Lying tangled amid the rumpled sheets, Ashley registered the lazy approbation of Jack's smoky-eyed gaze as he stroked a lazy finger from collar-bone to breast. Was this how every woman felt when she was in bed with a man she had grown to love? As if she were ten feet tall and could climb mountains without getting out of breath? Luxuriously, she stirred. 'How about something beginning with "S"?'

His hand continued its erotic journey. 'Not more sex?' he questioned with a mocking smile. 'Are you completely insatiable?'

'Why?' Ashley's eyes widened. How quickly she had learnt to play the bedroom games of flirtation. Just as she had learned all the other things her experienced lover had taught her. 'Don't you like me being insatiable?'

He circled a still-puckered nipple. 'I wouldn't have it any other way. You are the most assiduous...' his mouth now drifted to the rosy tip itself and he felt another great tug of desire '…pupil—that any man could wish for.'

'Am I?'

'Mmm.'

Ashley gave a sigh of pleasure as his lips worked their particular magic. And he was the most perfect teacher that any woman could ask for. He had taught her that sex could be many things: it could be urgent, lazy or infinitely tender. Jack Marchant wasn't so much her dream man—he exceeded every fantasy she'd ever had. She'd never thought she'd find herself initiated into the art of love-making by someone who was so uniquely passionate and intense. Who could make her want him the moment he looked at her. She'd never imagined that she would be the lover of a fabulously wealthy man and spend nights in his vast bed while the harsh wind from the moor keened outside the window.

It was a relationship which had made her blossom in every way—and hadn't she dared believe that their liaison had benefitted *him*, too? Because hadn't his haunted dreams of the past stopped happening? No more did he pace the corridors at night, locked in his own inner turmoil—instead he slept soundly, wrapped contentedly in her arms. And hadn't her own self-esteem grown as a result of that?

Tangling her fingers in the ruffled raven of his hair as she had longed to do countless times when she'd sat quietly working opposite him in his office, she snuggled closer. 'I was thinking we should get some fresh air, Jack,' she reflected. 'We should get up and go for a walk.

Just because it's winter doesn't mean we shouldn't make the most of the daylight—and we can't stay in bed all day.'

'Can't we? Can you give me one good reason why not?'

'Because sooner or later we need to eat something.'

'I'd like to eat *you*.' Jack buried his face in her neck, inhaling her wholesome soap-and-water scent and marvelling how everything with her seemed so *easy*. She wasn't constantly invading his space. Wanting to invade his mind, to know what he was thinking—and, more pertinently, to know what he was thinking about *her*. Against the softness of her firm skin, his eyes briefly closed. And shouldn't he thank whatever lucky stars he had that she didn't pry and question him? Because if she did...

Grimly, he blocked his thoughts and tightened his grip around her waist. He thought about the nightmares which had plagued him for so long that he hadn't been able to imagine life without them—and which had now gone. They'd been vanquished by the untroubled sleep he found with her. If he could put a price on the peace of mind he found in Ashley's arms, then wouldn't he happily forgo every penny of his vast fortune? 'So what would you *really* like to do today?'

For a moment, Ashley said nothing. Her face was buried in the warmth of his skin and so any wistfulness in her expression was shielded from him. He had just asked the million-dollar question and self-preservation meant that she was unable to answer it honestly. What she'd like most of all would be to be open about her relationship with Jack. Not to have to hide it away as if it was some kind of guilty secret and pretend it simply wasn't happening.

At times, it felt crazy—this subterfuge he had insisted on. Like when Christine was around and Ashley was terrified that a stray word or gesture might alert the housekeeper to the fact that she had become so much more than a secretary to her boss. And Jack didn't want that. Most definitely he didn't. He'd told her that from day one and nothing which had happened since had indicated that he'd changed his mind.

Ashley tried to tell herself that his wishes were understandable. Christine had worked for Jack and his family for many years. There were gardeners and cleaners employed at Blackwood, too—and it might reflect badly on *him* if he was seen as having 'seduced' his secretary. And it could be professional death for her.

So she forced herself to be pragmatic—to accept that the relationship might not last beyond the termination of her contract. Resolutely, she pushed all her worries to the back of her mind. She would enjoy what they had now—and not taint it with unrealistic yearnings. Instead, she tried to put a positive spin on it. It was *their* secret—something wonderful which was shared only by them and which the rest of the world couldn't intrude on.

She pressed her lips against the lobe of his ear. 'If you really want to know…I'd like to go for a long walk and then I'd like to have a bath—'

'Together?'

'If you think the bath is big enough, Jack.'

'I think we may have to cling very closely together. Or double up. You might *just* have to climb on top.'

'Oh, I think I could just about bear that.'

He laughed. 'And then?'

'Then I'd like to watch some soppy film and eat popcorn—and before you say that you don't like soppy films, I know that already. But you did ask me what I'd really like to do, Jack—and now I've told you.'

He was thoughtful for a moment and then he nodded his head. 'Okay.'

Surprised, she turned her face up to him. 'Just like that?'

'Why not?'

'If I'd known you were going to be so amenable, I'd have asked for more.'

He stilled—and thought in that moment that he'd have given her the world if it had been within his power to do so. *But it isn't, is it? You know it isn't.* 'And what else would you have asked for, Ashley?' he questioned softly.

She felt the race of her pulse. His love? His heart? 'Oh, a bar of chocolate as well!'

He smiled as he swung his legs over the edge of the bed and reached for his jeans. 'It's yours.'

Outside, the day was bitter and as they walked beneath a pewter sky Ashley thought that the moors had never looked more wild or more brooding. And neither had Jack, she realised as she stood beside him, the wind

whipping his raven hair and emphasising the height-
ened colour of his high cheekbones. What went through
that keen mind of his when he stared so fiercely at the
stark horizon? she wondered. And was that occasional
glimpse of savage pain she sometimes surprised on his
face provoked by memories of army life?

The bath which followed their walk was as protracted
as she'd hoped. She giggled as he soaped every inch of
her body and then washed her hair with slow fascina-
tion, and afterwards Jack left her drying her hair while
he drove into the village to hire a DVD. Ashley heard
his car pulling away and thought how weirdly *normal*
this all felt. And how perfect.

Too perfect? she wondered. Or was she just indulg-
ing in that leftover habit from childhood? Imagining a
worst-case scenario to toughen herself up just in case it
actually happened.

She dressed, went downstairs and lit the fire—but
when Jack returned her heart gave a little leap of anxiety
as she saw the expression on his face.

'Is something wrong?'

There was a pause. 'I ran into Christine.'

'Oh?'

'She looked a little surprised to see me carrying a
copy of *Bridget Jones's Diary* and a large packet of
salted popcorn.'

'Yes, I can imagine she might be. What did you
say?'

'I didn't *say* anything,' he answered coolly as he

handed her the film. 'I don't have to explain myself to anyone—least of all to my housekeeper.'

Ashley felt an unfamiliar tension invade the atmosphere as his sudden haughtiness seem to reinforce all the differences between them—until the more disturbing thought occurred to her that Christine's suspicions might be alerted. And would her relationship with Jack end? Would he decide to put a stop to it before word got round and people began to gossip about them? *I don't want it to end*, she thought fiercely as she wrapped her arms tightly around his neck and reached up on tiptoe to kiss him. *I want this to continue for as long as it can.*

Jack held himself still for a moment—until the softness of her kiss made him dissolve, just the way it always did. 'Oh, Ashley,' he said roughly, just before he began to deepen the kiss. 'I don't deserve you.'

She strived for just the right, light touch. 'Maybe you don't,' she mused.

They settled themselves down for the evening. *Bridget Jones* was one of Ashley's favourite films—but she quickly discovered that its plot failed to captivate when a man like Jack Marchant was making love to you on the sofa. Afterwards he carried her upstairs and slowly undressed her and then propped himself up on one elbow, looking at her naked body as she lay on the moon-washed bed.

'You are an amazing woman, do you know that?'

'I'm not anything special, Jack.'

He shook his head. She was wrong—but could he blame her for thinking it? If she was special then he wouldn't insist on secrecy. And after seeing the narrow-eyed look on his housekeeper's face earlier that evening, surely the need for secrecy was now academic...

He was still thoughtful next morning and when Ashley woke she began to make wordless and urgent love to him—and he gave a laugh of delight as he twisted her beneath him.

Afterwards, she leaned over him, her hair tickling his face. 'That was the most gorgeous thing in the world,' she whispered.

'You say that every time.'

'That's because it's true.' She hesitated. 'You're a wonderful lover, Jack.'

He heard the soft tremor of truth in her voice and her slight hesitation—and yet her shyness made the compliment more profound than any he'd ever been given before. She was so sweet, he thought suddenly. So soft and gentle. He had never known such moments of contentment as these spent lying in her arms—or imagined that he might ever find this kind of peace. So what was he going to do about it? he wondered with a sharp pang of conscience. For a while, he lay looking up at the ceiling—before getting out of bed and going over to take something from the small safe his lawyers insisted he keep.

Sleepily, Ashley watched him, remembering the blue scarf she had once found tucked away in a walnut bureau and which she had never asked him about. But that moment had long gone and, besides, it no longer seemed important. The only thing which mattered was this incredible thing they had between them. Was it love? On her part, certainly—but Jack never, ever gave his feelings away. Maybe that was yet another legacy of army life. And suddenly all her thoughts were forgotten as Jack approached, holding something tightly within his clenched hand.

He sat down on the edge of the bed and looked at her. 'I have something I want to give you, Ashley.'

The expression on his face made her heart skip a beat. It was a look she could never have described if she had lived to be a hundred and wouldn't have dared to—just in case she had misread it. She looked down at his fist. 'Wh-what is it?'

'This.' Slowly, his fingers unfurled to reveal a ring lying in the very centre of his palm. A rectangular diamond, surrounded by a glittering band of smaller stones and set in platinum. It was an old-fashioned ring—and it might not have been to everybody's taste, but Ashley loved it on sight. She stared up into his face.

'It belonged to my mother,' he said in answer to her unspoken question. 'And I want you to have it.'

Ashley swallowed. 'Why?' she whispered.

'Can't you guess why?'

'I can try, Jack—but I'm worried that it might be the wrong guess. A ring is a…strange present to give a lover,' she added shakily. 'Even I, with my scant experience of the opposite sex, know that it's a gesture which could so easily be misinterpreted.'

'I don't think there can be any misinterpretation in this case.' He reached across and took her hand in his.

'But just to make entirely sure that you understand... what if I told you that I love you, and that some day I want to marry you? That you have rebuilt my troubled soul brick by brick and that I can't contemplate life without you?'

His quietly passionate words felled her and she stared at him as if waiting for him to burst out laughing and tell her that it was nothing but a joke and that the ring was really from a cracker. But the expression in his black eyes was deadly serious. 'Jack—' But she was trembling so much that she couldn't continue.

'You're shocked?'

'Of course I'm shocked.'

'But not surprised, surely? And before you answer that, Ashley—just think about it. Ask yourself whether we don't seem to fit each other like a hand inside a glove. Whether the term soulmates—which up until recently I'd always scorned—shouldn't be applied to us. It's been like that between us from the very beginning— that sense of looking into someone's eyes and feeling as if you've suddenly come home. Hasn't it?'

Ashley nodded. She was having to swallow very hard in an attempt to hang onto her composure, and she looked down at the ring—afraid to meet his burning gaze for fear that she would dissolve and make a fool of herself. Because hadn't his words crystallised all her wishes and dreams—the ones she'd kept hidden, even from herself? Hadn't they given her a glimpse of some happy world which she knew existed but which she'd never felt part of before? Not until now. Now she could dare to dream.

'Oh, Jack,' she whispered. 'It's the most beautiful thing I've ever seen—but I don't need a ring to love you. You see, I think I've always loved you.'

'Sweet Ashley.' Even her words of love were more generous than he deserved. He took her hand and rubbed its palm with his thumb so that the urge to lift her eyes to his was irresistible. 'Totally without guile or artifice. Strong and dignified in spite of everything which fate has thrown at you. Don't you know how much I admire your spirit? Your ability to speak the truth without fear and your remarkable powers of calm—you who can soothe a man with one gentle look, or one soft and serene smile.'

'Jack,' she breathed.

'I love you,' he said simply. 'And I want to marry you.'

For a moment, she was speechless—her eyes searching his face.

'Do you think you could bear to be my wife?' he continued softly.

Her mouth was working but no words seemed to be coming and then she nodded, and her words seemed to fall over themselves in their eagerness to be heard. She, Ashley Jones who could never find a foster family to love her, was being proposed to by Jack Marchant? He was telling her that he loved her and wanted to spend the rest of his life with her. Was she dreaming—or was this really happening? 'Yes, oh yes! I mean, I do. Of course I'll marry you. How could I not when I love you so much? I can't…I can't believe… Oh, Jack!'

He slid the ring onto her finger—and then kissed her trembling lips.

'You're happy?' he asked.

'I'm beyond happy…I'm…ecstatic. It feels like a dream. Oh, Jack.'

'There's just one thing.' He lifted her hand to his mouth and kissed it. 'I don't want you to tell anybody else about this. Do you understand? Not just yet.'

Her bubble of happiness wobbled as she saw the diamond's light reflected on his lips. 'Is there…a particular reason why?'

'It's complicated. Can you trust me, Ashley?'

There was a pause. Yes, she could trust him. If she had given him her heart then she *had* to trust him. *Not just yet*, he had said. And surely she could understand that. He was a fiercely private man and this was to be theirs. Theirs alone—nobody else's.

'Does that mean I shouldn't wear the ring?' she questioned.

'Well, not as a general rule, no—not yet. How about only wearing it in the bedroom?' he murmured as he bent to kiss her. 'Let's say it's the *only* thing you're allowed to wear in the bedroom.'

It seemed a reasonable—and provocative—request. And, of course, Ashley adapted to the situation because she *wanted* to. Just as she wanted him—more than she had ever wanted anything. If she'd been older or wiser, she might have questioned his request and asked herself why he was so intent on keeping it a secret from the world. But Ashley was too blinded by love and excitement to care. Each morning, she would hold her hand up to the light to stare at the ring—where the ice-white dazzle of the stone reminded her that this *wasn't* all a figment of her imagination.

Maybe it was happiness which made her careless…

Jack had gone down to London for a couple of days to meet with his literary agent and his lawyers, leaving Ashley behind to work on the manuscript. He didn't ask her to accompany him and she didn't expect him to—but it was the first time they'd been parted since they'd become lovers and she missed him desperately. She continued to sleep in his bed, even though she hated the empty space beside her. And she would press her face into his pillow, breathing in his distinctive scent and longing for the time when he would be home.

At least having the place to herself meant that she could get on with her work. Uninterrupted in the quiet house, she made huge inroads into his book and was tackling chapter ten when Christine walked into the office one morning. Ashley looked up in surprise. 'Christine!'

'Why, you look like you've seen a ghost,' observed the housekeeper.

'B-but you're not supposed to be here!'

'There's been a package delivered to the post office for Mr Marchant and they rang to ask me to collect it as they couldn't get a reply from here. Perhaps I should have run it past you first?' said Christine with a slight edge of sarcasm in her voice.

With a sudden lurch of her heart, Ashley realised that she was still wearing her ring and quickly she slid her hand onto her lap. Had the other woman seen it? And would it be obvious if she started trying to tug the ring off underneath her desk? Oh, this was *insane*. Why had Jack done this? she wondered with a sudden rare burst of anger. Did he mean to make her feel as if she was not only an object of affection but also one of shame?

'I didn't mean to sound rude, Christine.'

'Of course you didn't.' The housekeeper hesitated for a moment, and then she pulled a funny kind of face. 'Perhaps you ought to know that people round here are beginning to talk.'

'Talk?' Ashley stilled. 'What do you mean exactly?'

'These small villages are hotbeds of gossip—and word gets around. One of the cleaners has been talking about you—saying that you and Mr Marchant seem very...'

'Very what?'

'Close.'

Don't react, Ashley told herself as she surreptitiously slid the ring from her finger and let her fingers close round it. 'Well, we *do* work closely together.'

There was an awkward pause. 'You're a nice little thing, Ashley—and I'd hate to see you hurt.' Christine's face grew pink. 'Just remember that the rich don't always have it easy—and it's not all it's cracked up to be. They have their secrets and their troubles, too.'

Ashley wanted to ask what she meant—but how could she possibly do that when she was sitting with the claws of the precious diamond ring digging into her palm? To start discussing such a contentious subject with Christine would surely lay her open to all kinds of complications—and weren't things already complicated enough?

'I'll try to remember that,' she said lightly.

But Christine's words brought all her insecurities flaring into life. *I'd hate to see you hurt*, the housekeeper had said. Did that mean that she had witnessed this kind of scenario before, watching as a stream of secretaries were seduced by Jack and then cast aside when he'd tired of them?

No. Ashley's lips tightened. She didn't believe that—not for a minute. He wasn't the kind of man to do something like that—some bone-deep instinct told her that, though she couldn't have said why. People talked because they loved to create a scandal. And if they wanted to gossip because they suspected that a lowly secretary was having an affair with the rich and aristocratic Jack Marchant—then let them. Perhaps it might even do them both a favour. Mightn't it be better if it all came out into the open—so that they wouldn't have to keep behaving in this furtive way?

When he came back from London, she would talk to him about it. Tell him that she loved him but was uneasy about all this secrecy—and hope that he agreed with her.

He was due in at six and she prepared for his return in a high state of excitement. She spent ages drying her hair and she left it loose—so that it fell in a shining caramel curtain over her shoulders. Then she put on a simple cream woollen dress, which hugged at hip and breast. Her only adornment was her diamond ring—and its icy brilliance sparkled on her finger.

She heard his key in the door and rushed to meet him. Flakes of snow clung to his raven hair and his rugged face looked taut and strained, she thought. 'Jack,' she said softly.

'Did you miss me?' he growled.

'Desperately.'

He gave a low and unsteady laugh. When he'd been away he had half wondered if he had been imagining the solace and the passion he had found in her arms. But one moment in her company made him realise that it was all true. 'Then come here and kiss me.'

'I thought you'd never ask.'

The kiss became protracted.

'I've missed you, too,' he groaned.

'Show me how much,' she whispered.

He took her upstairs and made love to her on the bed where she'd slept alone during his absence. But he seemed pent-up, she thought as he pulled the clothes from her body with fingers which were unsteady. And Ashley clung to him with a fierce fervour as he lowered his head and began to kiss her.

'Was it a good trip?' she questioned much later, when they had dressed again and were sitting on the rug in front of the library fire, drinking red wine and feeding each other peanuts.

For a moment Jack said nothing as he looked down into her wide-spaced green eyes. Was now the moment to tell her about the long and uncomfortable meeting he'd had with his lawyer—and all the obstacles which lay ahead of them? But at least he had discovered that there was a way out. A way forward. He pulled her into his arms. 'It was a useful trip.'

'Oh?'

He was going to have to tell her, Jack realised as he recognised that she had already proved her worth. Hadn't her reluctance to pry into his life shown him that he could trust her—and that maybe now was the time to show her just how much? He smoothed the soft and newly washed hair away from her face as he came up against a cold wall of reluctance. Couldn't it wait until morning—when he had spent one last and care-free night in her arms? Or was that just putting off the inevitable?

'There's something I need to talk to you about, Ashley—'

The heaviness of his tone made her feel a sudden quickening beat of misgiving but just as Ashley began to frame her question the doorbell rang and so she replaced it with another one.

'Who on earth's that at this time of night?' she whispered.

'I don't know,' he growled. 'Let's just ignore it.'

They sat in silence for a moment while they waited for the caller to go away, but after a short pause the ringing began again.

Uncomfortably, Ashley shifted on the mat. 'It might be important.'

'In that case, then why didn't they telephone first?'

With echoing persistence, the doorbell sounded through the house and Ashley bit her lip. 'We'll have to answer it, Jack. They can see the lights on and must know we're in. Look, I'll go and take a message and get rid of them.'

He let her go and afterwards he thought that was the stupidest thing he had ever done. In bare feet, her journey through the house was quiet but he heard the heavy door creaking open and then the sound of low voices.

Now he heard footsteps—heavy and deliberate. And then the sight of Ashley, white-faced with confusion as she led in a man with tanned skin, a too-light suit and an expression of simmering fury.

Jack rose to his feet and his body tensed. 'What the hell are you doing here?'

'So here you are, Marchant—long time no see,' interrupted the man, in a low American accent. 'Seems like I'm interrupting something. Seems like the rumours I heard were all true. You should be careful if you start leading a double life, Jack—because word gets around. The internet's made that kind of easy. Surely you know that?' His mouth curved into an odd smile as he looked around. 'Cosy little love nest you've got,' he observed. 'I knew you were rich, of course, but it's always interesting to get confirmation.'

By the shafts of his thighs, Jack's hands curled into tight fists. 'What do you want?'

'You know damned well what I want.' The man's eyes flicked to Ashley. 'Though maybe the little lady doesn't. Are you going to tell her, or am I?'

'T-tell me what?' demanded Ashley, her voice shaking as some sixth sense seemed to tell her that her happy new world was about to come crashing down around her.

The man's gaze alighted on the diamond ring she wore. 'Has Jack asked you to marry him?' he drawled. 'Because if he has—you might be advised to see a lawyer before you give him your answer.'

'I d-don't know what you're talking about,' said Ashley, her heart racing so fast that the sound of the man's voice sounded distorted.

'Then maybe I should enlighten you. You see, your lover is already married, sweetheart,' he said. 'To my sister. And there's no way you can become Mrs Marchant when she still has that title. Bigamy might be rare these days but it's still a pretty big no-no where society is concerned.'

For the first time, Ashley looked at Jack properly, her heart crashing against her ribcage, not wanting to believe a word this intruder had said. And then her hopes died as she realised it was. For the truth was written on every pore of his face—from the pain which clouded the brilliant black eyes to the tight, hard line of his mouth.

And suddenly everything clicked into place. The gossip in the village. Christine's awkwardness—did Christine *know*? But most of all…Jack's own inexplicable desire for secrecy. Tell a woman you loved her and that you wanted to marry her and then tell her that it was a big secret. She hadn't known why and she'd been too scared to dig deep and now she knew exactly why he had made that demand.

Jack Marchant was already married!

Somehow she began to move on legs which were threatening to buckle beneath her. She made her way towards the door—aware of nothing other than the terrible pain in her heart and an overpowering sense of shock and betrayal.

He had lied and cheated his way into her arms! Cold-bloodedly mounted a slow seduction which couldn't fail to be anything other than successful. He had taken her virginity and she had given it to him, gladly—because she had loved him. But more than that, she had dared to trust him—she who found it hard to trust anyone. She had given Jack her heart, and he had crushed it in his fist as if it was of no consequence!

Without another look, she passed the man with the American accent and her teeth were chattering as she made her way upstairs, her feet stumbling over the stairs which led up to her room. Once inside, she locked the door, resting her head against its surface, her shock and her distress so great that she slid to her knees on the floor.

And, burying her face in her trembling hands, she began to sob as if her heart were breaking.

CHAPTER ELEVEN

'ASHLEY? Will you please open this door?'

From behind its protective wooden sanctuary, Ashley heard the sound of Jack's voice. That was the voice she had once loved—which could veer between sarcasm and tenderness and which made her senses come to life. And wasn't the pitiful truth that, despite what he had told her, nothing had changed. She loved him still and she suspected she always would. Even his unbelievable betrayal was not, it seemed, enough to extinguish the feelings she had for him. Once before he had stood behind her door and made the very same request that she open it. But that time she had not locked it—and that time she had not been in deep enough to have her heart broken into a million pieces. Now she was—and she had only her own stupid self to blame.

'Ashley—for God's sake, will you at least *answer* me—just to let me know that you're okay?'

'What do you want me to say, Jack?'

'I don't care what you say, just say something. Call

me every name under the sun if it will make you feel
better.'

She gave a bitter laugh. He thought *that* would make
her feel better? 'What good would that do?' she questioned tiredly.

'Look, I don't want to have this conversation with a
door between us, Ashley. So will you open it…please?
I'm not going to go away until you do—and if you per-
sist in locking me out then I just may be tempted to kick
the damned thing open.'

Would he have done that? Ashley didn't know—
or, rather, she didn't feel in any fit position to judge
what he would or wouldn't do. Not any more. Had she
known him at all, she wondered—or had the Jack she
had fallen in love with been nothing but a figment of her
own imagination? Had she seen only what she'd wanted
to see—while blinding herself to the truth? He was a
married man, she reminded herself bitterly. He already
had a wife and yet he had blithely been proposing that
he share his future with *her*. He had spun her a load of
romantic fantasies—and she had fallen under his spell
and accepted them as reality.

But he was right. She was going to have to face him
some time—and either she endured a long and sleepless night or she had it out with him now. And besides,
Christine would be here in the morning—and how could
they possibly discuss it then? No wonder he had been so
adamant he wanted to keep the whole affair a secret, she
thought. Had Christine known of his marital state—and

if she had, then why had she never mentioned it to her before?

Because she wouldn't have dared. Christine would have known as a housekeeper that it would be overstepping the mark to question her employer's morality with his lover. Jack held all the power, Ashley realised. He could do what the hell he wanted—simply because of who he was. He held it even now…*open the door or he would be tempted to kick it down*. Wasn't that just another example of the arrogant aristocrat wanting his own way?

Slowly, she opened the door and saw him standing there, taken aback by the haunted look which had turned his face to a tortured mask—but she tried to harden her heart against it. She saw him glance over her shoulder to the bed behind her and a muscle tightened at his jaw.

'We can't talk here,' he said abruptly.

Once she might have teased him about the bed and the temptation it offered—but those days were gone.

'No, we can't,' she agreed flatly.

'Put on something warm and come downstairs. You look half frozen.'

She glanced down at her goose-bumped arms. She *was* cold—freezing cold, come to think of it—and she hadn't even noticed. 'I'll be down in a minute,' she said.

For a moment he seemed to hesitate, and that was so unlike the Jack she knew—because when did *he* ever hesitate about anything?

'Okay—but don't be long,' he said tersely.

Pulling a thick sweater on over the cream dress she had worn for his homecoming, she went downstairs to where Jack had lit the fire. He looked up as she walked in.

'Please sit down, Ashley.'

Obediently, she sank down onto one of the velvet chairs, watching like a mute observer as he walked over to the drinks trolley, splashed some brandy into a glass and came back and handed it to her.

'I don't like brandy.'

'Drink it, Ashley,' he said fiercely. 'Your face is so white I'm wondering whether there's any blood left in your veins.'

She *felt* bloodless, too—as if all the vibrant life of earlier had left her, never to return again. But she sipped the brandy and felt some of the warmth return.

He stared at her as she drank and she was aware of that burning gaze—as if he was committing her to memory. And maybe she was doing the same as she studied him back—filing away the image of that beloved face so that in some distant future she might be able to take it out and look at it without her heart breaking into tiny pieces.

His face was still dark and his voice distorted with some kind of painful emotion as he spoke. 'So? No questions, Ashley? No accusations? No rightful fury hurled at me for my deception?'

Fury? Didn't he realise that fury would be a preferable alternative to this terrible tearing pain which was tearing at her heart? 'What would be the point? It's true, isn't it?'

'Yes, it's true.' His mouth tightened. 'Don't you want to hear my story?'

'Why, will it change the facts, Jack? That you had a wife? *Have* a wife,' she corrected painfully. 'It's usually something a man mentions to a woman—especially when he tells her he loves her and wants to marry her.'

'Shall I tell you about my wife, Ashley? Shall I?' he demanded. He was fired up now, a muscle working furiously in his cheek as he stood in front of the fire— so that the flare of the orange flames flickered behind him. 'You know those bad dreams I sometimes have.'

'The ones which used to make you pace the corridors?' she questioned shakily. 'The ones you never wanted to discuss?' That had been something *else* he had kept locked away from her, she thought, realising that maybe she'd never known him at all. Just thought she had...

'I didn't want to discuss them because the past was something I wanted to forget—just as you prefer to forget yours. When I was with you, all I was concerned about was the present.'

But the past affected the present, Ashley realised as she stared at him. 'When did the dreams start?'

'Soon after I was discharged from the army, when I first returned to civilian life. At first, I barely slept a wink. I couldn't get used to being in a bed. I felt caged by four walls. I thought I would never know peace again. I was shell-shocked. Literally…'

His voice tailed off and Ashley couldn't help her heart's automatic leap of sympathy as she saw the tortured expression on his face. *But his war record is not the thing in question here*, she told herself fiercely. *His marriage is.*

'The dreams started to come nightly,' he continued. 'With cruel clarity they replayed scenes straight from hell—which took me straight back to the war zone. They spilled over into my days and I couldn't seem to settle to anything. Apparently, it's not an uncommon scenario for military personnel who've been engaged in active combat. I had a manager running the estates here and no pressing money worries which tied me to any one place. I'd bought some real estate in America before I'd taken up my commission and so I decided to combine a post-service holiday to Santa Barbara with a look at some of my properties there—before I decided what I wanted to do with my future.'

So far so good, Ashley thought as she put her empty brandy glass down, but she didn't risk herself to speak. How could she when she knew what he was about to tell her?

'I don't suppose you've ever seen pictures of Santa Barbara?' he questioned. 'It's an idyllic little place— as if somebody from Central Casting had gone there and slapped down a perfect beach town on the west coast of the United States. The ocean is amazing and the vegetation was like nothing I'd ever seen before.

Blossom trees grow side by side with lush and exotic plants. Every blade on every lawn is clipped and every street is clean. It was warm and it was beautiful and I rented a house on a place called Hope Ranch—and the name seemed somehow symbolic after everything I'd been through. I could see ocean and mountains from my windows and there was a pool where I could swim every morning before breakfast.'

He sounded as if he were quoting from a travel brochure, thought Ashley—but still she said nothing.

'To some extent, it worked. The rest and the beauty helped heal me but I guess deep down I was lonely and my experiences had left me craving company, and comfort. There was a realty agent who was showing me some of my properties and she happened to be blonde, and fun. For a while she was able to make me forget the horrors I'd seen, and, well, we became…close.' He sighed. 'It should never have been anything more than an affair—but somehow it didn't quite work out that way. Because one day Kelly announced she was pregnant.'

Ashley bit back a gasp of horror. Did the story of his past have even greater ramifications than she'd thought? Did Jack also have a *child*?

'So we married,' he continued, ignoring the blanched expression on her face—unwilling to halt the painful telling of his story in case he couldn't bring himself to start again. 'Only it turned out that the pregnancy wasn't real. It was a classic case of entrapment, only I was still too blitzed to have seen through it—and too much of a gentleman to ask to see the test results. But we were

married and I was at an age to start thinking about settling down and so I thought…maybe this *can* work. And
then, I have to *make* it work. Pride made me want my
marriage to be a success. I gave it my best shot—I really
did—but we were completely unsuited. We wanted different things out of life. Kelly liked spending my money,
going to glitzy parties and flying from city to city. The
life she craved was just one big adult playground, and
that wasn't me at all. I began to miss my home—the
emptiness of the moors and the low English skies. I
couldn't see myself settling in the States and she took
one look at a photo of Blackwood and refused to ever
set foot in the place.'

'So what happened?' breathed Ashley.

'I broached the subject of a separation and that's
when she started making astronomical alimony de-
mands. Crazy stuff.' He gave a hollow kind of laugh.
'She wanted millions of dollars for a marriage which
had lasted less than six months. I told her that while I
would be fair, I had no intention of being stitched up.
We were driving back towards Hope Ranch one day
when she lost her temper and suddenly started hitting
at me, and when that had no effect—she tried to grab
the steering wheel.'

For a moment there was a long, strained silence
and Ashley looked at him with a question in her eyes
even though deep down she already knew the bleak
answer.

'We crashed,' he finished baldly.

Ashley winced. 'Crashed?'

'We hit one of the tall palm trees they call "widow makers". Kelly nearly didn't make it—she sustained a brain injury and they operated on her that day. And when she came round from the anaesthetic, she was in a coma. A deep, vegetative state, the doctors called it.' He swallowed. 'In which she remains to this day.'

'Oh, my God. Oh, how awful. Oh, Jack—I'm so sorry! How long…I mean, how long has it been?' she whispered.

'Two years.'

Two years? Suddenly, Ashley felt as if her life were a jigsaw puzzle which somebody had just snatched up and shaken all over the floor.

He gave a ragged sigh as he stared at her. 'I know what you must be thinking, Ashley—that I'm heartless and cruel and deceitful, and, yes, maybe I am. But I sat by her bedside for weeks while they conducted test after test. Weeks became months. I had every top specialist flown in and they all said the same thing. That it was hopeless, that she would never recover—and that I should go away and live my own life. For a while I refused to believe them. I said that there were such things as miracles—but I was wrong. No miracle ever happened and eventually I took their advice and came home. But I wasn't planning on meeting someone else and falling in love with her—nor on wanting to spend the rest of my life with her.'

But words which would once have thrilled her had lost their power to move. 'Why didn't you tell me this before?'

'And when should I have done that?' he demanded. 'From the moment I met you it was already too late. My guard was down because I never imagined that someone like you would pose any threat. You were too young and too gauche—you simply weren't my type. And then I began to notice the person you really were underneath. One who was honest and spirited and yet shy all at the same time. Who had all the qualities I'd never dreamed a woman could have. You just bewitched me, Ashley, and I was imprisoned by your spell. I kept saying to myself—I will tell her today. And then, no, I will tell her tomorrow. And then tomorrow became tomorrow. There was always another tomorrow. And then, of course—we became lovers—'

'Adulterous lovers,' she breathed, her faced flushed with a combination of shame and brandy as she stared at him.

Uncomfortably, he shrugged. 'In theory.'

'No, Jack—in practice,' she insisted and then shook her head, her heart as heavy as lead. 'Why give me the ring? Why make the proposal?' she demanded. 'Was that your own form of entrapment? Of pretending that none of your past life had ever happened?'

'And haven't you ever pretended?' he snapped, his face suddenly darkening with a fierce kind of anger. 'That the world is not like it *really* is, but a Utopian version which is kind to us all?'

She stared at him. 'Of course I have,' she answered slowly. She, more than anyone, had spent her whole childhood fantasising about being someone else who lived somewhere else. Pretending that she had a mother and father who loved her and a safe and cosy little house somewhere in the suburbs. 'And you're right—I can't heap all the blame on you. I pretended to myself that everything was fine between us when deep down I knew there was something wrong. There were lots of unanswered questions and things that weren't quite right. Things I didn't dare confront because maybe I wanted the Utopian version, too. So maybe I was guilty of cowardice for not having confronted the issue.'

She remembered something else now. Something else which she had blocked. 'There's a scarf tucked away in your study,' she said slowly. 'A beautiful blue scarf, shot with gold.'

His face was ashen now and his voice sounded tortured. 'It belonged to Kelly,' he said. 'She was wearing it on the day of the crash. The hospital gave it to me and I brought it home. Every time I looked at it, I thought of her lying stricken and unresponsive in her hospital bed. I could hardly bear to keep it, and yet I couldn't bring myself to throw it away.'

'Oh, Jack.'

His mouth hardened, as if her quiet words of automatic sympathy had only added to his pain. 'Can't you see that the moment I told you about my past, it would have coloured it black?' he appealed. 'The way it's doing right now. Maybe I just wanted to experience the joy of telling the woman I love that I wanted to spend the rest of my life with her—without this dark reality pressing down on us. Was that such a terrible thing to do, Ashley—to chase that brief moment of joy?'

'Yes. No. I *don't know*, Jack.'

He moved away from the fire and walked towards her and in spite of everything she could feel herself tremble with love as he grew closer.

'This doesn't have to change anything, you know,' he said.

Her heart thumping she stared up at him. 'Are you out of your mind?'

'Why should it? Kelly is getting the best treatment in the world and that will never change. I will continue to care for her in every way that I can. You and I could carry on being lovers—just as before. But if you want, I will divorce her. That's one of the reasons I went down to London to see my lawyer—to find out where I stood legally, and—'

'No!'

Her fierce response must have taken him by surprise because he stopped, his black eyes narrowing as he stared back at her.

'You once told me you could forgive me anything,' he said slowly.

'And at the time I meant it—but I was wrong. I can't pretend that everything's hunky-dory. Don't you see this is hopeless? That it must all end?' she whispered. 'I can't be your lover any more, Jack—and I can't put myself in the way of temptation. I have to go away from here—far away. We have to forget all about each other and everything we've been to each other, don't you see that?'

'But why, Ashley? *Why?*'

She shook her head. Couldn't he see? Was he going to make her endure yet more pain by having to spell it out for him word by aching word? 'Because it's wrong—and I can't do it. I can't bear the thought of you divorcing a sick and helpless woman because of me—and neither can I bear the thought of sharing your bed while she's still alive. But it's more than that, Jack—it's the whole trust thing. You should have told me and you didn't tell me—and I don't think...' Her voice faltered slightly before the words came rushing out in a bitter stream. 'I don't think I would ever be able to trust you again. That trust has been broken and I don't think it can ever be mended. And whichever way you look at it—that's no basis for married life or any other kind of life together.'

He flinched then as if she had hit him, staring into her face for a long moment before abruptly turning away from her and going over to stare into the heart of the fire. And when he turned again, his face was changed. Different. So that for a moment he looked like a remote stranger and not like Jack at all.

'I'm asking you to sleep on it. Not to make any decisions in the heat of the moment,' he said. 'I will not attempt to influence you in any way other than to emphasise that what we share is rare. You know it is, Ashley. What has happened has been one almighty mess which I could have—and should have—handled better.

But the fundamental facts haven't changed. I love you and you love me—and I'm a lot older than you are. I've been around a bit and I've seen the way things work in this crazy world of ours.' His voice lowered into an urgent entreaty. 'Let me assure you that this kind of love doesn't come along very often. We're *compatible*, you and I—we both know that. We have something which is special. And that if we let it go…if we squander it… well, we'd be crazy.'

She thought if that was Jack *not* influencing her, then she would like to hear what he had to say when he *was*. Though on second thoughts, maybe she wouldn't. Because wasn't it difficult enough now to resist the urge to fling herself into his arms and have him cover her hair and face with his hot, sweet kisses? To let his love-making banish all her doubts and her fears. They could never go back to the way it had been before, but surely they could find another way—one which would still take into account that rare compatibility he'd spoken of.

But could she live like that—knowing that their happiness would for ever be tarnished by another woman's tragedy? Ashley stared into Jack's black eyes, drinking in their gleaming brilliance and hoping that her face did not betray her tumultuous thoughts. Because if he had any idea of what was in her mind, wouldn't he try to stop her?

'I've listened to everything you've said,' she answered slowly. 'And now I'm going upstairs to bed.'

'Ashley—'

'Let me sleep on it,' she said. 'Please. Don't ask any

more than that.' And with that, she quickly left the room—before she broke down in front of him. Knowing that there was nothing to sleep on. The words she'd spoken to him had been true. It *was* going to have to end and she *was* going to have to leave. To go somewhere far away—where Jack could not find her and tempt her into coming back…

Sleep was out of the question. Instead, she lay wide-eyed on her bed until she heard his heavy footfall on the stairs and the clicking shut of his door. She waited until the house was completely silent before she crept around her room, quietly layering a few essential pieces of clothing into a small bag—listening out like a burglar for the sound of movement.

She tried writing a note—but could find no words for what she wanted to say. To berate him for having betrayed her and broken her heart would be unnecessarily cruel to a man who had surely suffered enough. To tell him that she had loved him and suspected she always would might give both of them false hope. Because she had spoken the truth earlier and they did *not* have any kind of future. Not together.

The diamond ring she slid from her finger and laid in the centre of the table by the window, where it winked reproachfully at her—a cold and precious symbol of all that would never be hers.

But it wasn't until dawn brought with it the concealing sound of birdsong that she made her way downstairs. Like a ghost, she slipped through the back door and as she did she heard the shrilling sound of the phone. Briefly, she wondered who on earth was ringing at this time of the morning—but the business of Blackwood was no longer her business. Quietly, she shut the door behind her and said a silent goodbye to her old life.

Skirting the main lawns, she was soon swallowed up by the trees which bordered the lane. The light was pearly grey and it was a chill morning, but Ashley didn't notice anything other than the frantic beat of her heart and the urgent need to get away. Far away—even though something seemed to be pulling her back towards the black-eyed man who probably was not asleep either...

She'd thought about what Jack might do if some sixth sense alerted him to her absence and sent him running after her. The nearest railway station was the first place he'd look. So she carried on walking—her ears alert to the sound of approaching cars...or horses... And only when she'd put several miles between herself and Blackwood, did she risk sliding her mobile phone from the pocket of her jeans and dialling a taxi company.

The cab arrived twenty minutes later and she slid onto the back seat.

'Where to?' questioned the driver as he looked at her in the rear mirror.

Ashley swallowed. Where to? Where could she run to and seek refuge? London, she guessed. She had friends there and it was big enough and anonymous enough to lose herself if Jack should try to find her.

She leaned forward to speak to the driver while

outside the sun struggled to break through a heavy grey sky and nothing but an empty future seemed to lie ahead of her.

CHAPTER TWELVE

LONDON looked different and it felt different, too. After the wildness of the moors and the pure, clean air the city seemed to crowd in on her. As she alighted from the train Ashley could see people everywhere—and she wondered if they could read the bitter heartache written on her face.

She had friends in London—friends who would have willingly taken her in and given her a sofa to sleep on. Who would have opened a bottle of wine—or two—and told her that there were plenty more fish in the sea and she would soon get over Jack Marchant.

But Ashley knew it wasn't as easy as that. Just as she knew that she couldn't face any of her friends—no matter how well intentioned they might be. Her grief was too big and intense and personal to allow anyone else to intrude on it. And her feelings for Jack were too complicated by love. *She* might silently curse him for having broken her heart—but she wouldn't allow other people to do the same.

So she checked into one of the small hotels which

could be found tucked away in the less salubrious parts of every city, and there she curled herself up in a soulless room, on a narrow bed. For two days, she alternated between fitful sleep and tears, and existed on cups of hot, sweet tea made on a hissing little kettle which sat next to the TV.

By the third day, she knew she needed strength and went out to buy herself food—forcing herself to go to a café, where she ordered a plateful of bacon and eggs and hot, buttered toast. It was comfort food—and it had the desired effect. She ate every mouthful, knowing that afterwards she would feel better. Because Ashley was an old hand at recovery. She'd had setback after setback many times in her life, and every time she had managed to bounce back. It took effort—a big effort—and never had it seemed as difficult as it did this time. Her heart and her spirit had never felt this shattered before—but what choice did she have? To fade away and cease to exist? To become a shadow of a woman, letting her doomed love affair ruin the rest of her life?

No. She would never forget Jack and she didn't want to—but she had strived too hard in the past to allow herself to cave in now.

It was tempting to find a brand-new employment agency and to start all over again—but she'd worked for Julia at Trumps since she'd left school and she had a proven work record with them. And so she risked paying the office a visit. Would Jack have contacted them? she wondered. Told them that she'd behaved unprofessionally by walking out without giving notice—knowing that she would probably never dream of telling them the reason why?

But he had done no such thing. Her salary had been paid in full—right to the end of the contract—and he had even provided a glowing reference without being asked. And wasn't there a part of Ashley's spirit which sank when Julia passed on this particular piece of news? She had told him that it must end and that she didn't want to be contacted—but hadn't she thought that he might at least *try*?

And then what? Put herself through the torture of having to send him away—and make her heart break into a thousand pieces all over again?

Trumps Agency lived up to its name and quickly found her a live-in post, working for the general manager of a smart boutique hotel in a small Dorset town in the south of England. It was a pretty little place and the countryside was fairly tame when she compared it with the wild and rugged beauty of the moors. But Ashley wanted that. Maybe she needed that. She didn't need an untamed wildness which reminded her too poignantly of Jack. And this time she had the sea—with its ever-changing beauty and the endless sound of the waves, which soothed her troubled heart.

Two months into her new job and she discovered to her surprise that her smiles felt much less of an effort than they had done in those first early days of leaving Jack. But she'd known how important it was to keep smiling. If you didn't smile then people asked you questions. They wanted to know if you were miserable—and then why, and she hadn't wanted to answer that.

Ashley knew that life had to go on—and that time healed. She had to put her faith in all the old clichés which had always comforted people in times of trouble. So she did her new job as best she could. She was calm and efficient and her work seemed to please her boss—and at least spring had come at last. It brought with it all the fresh, bright bulbs bursting through the bare earth and filling the warm air with their delicate fragrance. And surely that boded well for her future? In time, wouldn't the changing of the seasons wash away more and more of the pain she felt at being parted from Jack?

She joined a French evening class and started taking swimming lessons at the local pool, and slowly began to make friends. Her life felt quiet and uneventful—but that was exactly what she wanted.

And then two things happened which changed her world. The first was that a lawyer contacted her through the employment agency and Julia said no, she didn't have a clue what it was about, but that there was a phone number for Ashley to ring.

Cautiously, Ashley did so—withholding her number and prepared to hang up if it was anything to do with Jack. But it was not. It was to do with her mother—or, rather, the family of her late mother who had decided that her neglected offspring must be traced.

It was strange, thought Ashley—as she sat opposite a well-spoken lawyer in his London office one afternoon—how death could sometimes help heal the quarrels of the living. Her maternal grandmother seemed to have been struck by a death-bed bout of guilt and remorse and had amended her will accordingly. She was determined in some small way to compensate the granddaughter she had failed to acknowledge during her lifetime. In fact, she was more than generous—and extremely wealthy. It transpired that Ashley had inherited a substantial amount of money—as well as an extended and scattered family who were curious to meet her.

The money was enough to ensure that Ashley could banish some of her uncertainty about her future. She would certainly need to keep working—but at least now she was going to be able to buy a property of her own. For the first time in her life she could afford a roof over her head—her own place at last. It was her first real experience of security and she discovered she liked it—and that it went a long way in helping her shake off some of her ingrained feelings of inferiority.

Her habitual reserve initially made her baulk at the thought of getting to know a whole batch of newly discovered relations—but the aching hole in her heart left by the end of her affair with Jack made her make a tentative move towards meeting them. A large family party followed—a confusing and noisy affair which left Ashley feeling faintly bemused. But to her surprise, she was welcomed into the fold and she quickly began to know and to love her little nieces and nephews. Her weekends now began to include occasional trips to Gloucestershire, where many of them were based—and having her own family gave her another unfamiliar taste of security, and of roots.

But the second thing which happened rocked Ashley's world far more than an unexpected inheritance. Another phone call arrived from the agency—with Julia moaning that she felt like her personal secretary—telling her that Christine had been in touch and was pleading with Ashley to ring her, urgently.

Ashley hesitated for only a moment because she knew that Jack wouldn't dream of asking his housekeeper to intervene on his behalf. He was much too proud for that—he could have tried himself through the agency and he hadn't done. So why was she wanted? Some instinct made fear swell up inside her stomach and grip at her throat. She stood in a quiet alcove at the boutique hotel as she gripped the phone, while a shaky-voiced Christine told her that there had been an accident.

'What kind of an accident?' demanded Ashley.

'A fire. A terrible fire. Ashley...' There was a kind of gulping sound, the sound of someone swallowing their tears. 'Blackwood has been destroyed.'

Ashley's knees buckled. The world threatened to cave in around her. 'And Jack? Was he hurt?'

There was a silence—a terrible, gathering silence.

'He was,' said Christine, her solid voice sounding precariously close to breaking. 'Badly hurt. He's blind, Ashley. Mr Marchant's blind.'

Blind? Her beloved Jack *blind*? Only some inner strength she didn't know she possessed stopped Ashley from falling to the ground—and from railing at a God who was clearly not listening. Sucking in a ragged breath, she steadied her breathing enough to ask, 'And where is he? Where is he now?'

'He's living in one of the other properties on the other side of the estate. You know the old Ivy House?'

'I do.'

'He's there. I still work for him. I go in most days now and he has…well, he has a couple of carers living in who help look after him.'

Carers? Her brave, strong Jack—the man who had been commended for bravery in all the active service he had seen—was being looked after by *carers*? Ashley swallowed down the acrid taste of horror as she tried to imagine the reality of his life. How on earth would such an independent man cope with having to rely on others for his very existence?

'Christine,' she said slowly. 'I'm coming to see him—but you must not tell him. You must not. That is imperative. Do you understand?'

'Yes, Ashley. I understand.'

Ashley went into the office to speak to her boss. He was a fair man who she hoped would let her go with his blessing—though she knew that she would leave without it, for she had no choice. 'I need to go urgently to see a dear friend who is very sick,' she said, in a low voice—the irony not escaping her that this was the second time she had failed to give adequate notice to her employer.

'And are you planning on coming back?'

'I don't know,' she said honestly—for wasn't honesty the only thing she had ever been able to rely on?

Something in her face made him treat her kindly, as though she herself were some kind of invalid, and Ashley made the long journey back north with nothing more than an overnight bag. The journey took hours—punctuated by delays at two railway stations and a train which seemed to rattle like a sack of bones. Her stomach was so churned up that she couldn't bear to eat anything—sipping only at weak, warm tea and unable to settle until at last the train drew into Stonecanton station.

She jumped into the waiting taxi and gave the driver directions and, if he looked at her curiously, she was too tired and too scared to satisfy his curiosity with any kind of explanation. Ivy House was on the western side of the estate but the taxi took her past Blackwood and, on an impulse, Ashley made the driver take the car up the long drive so that she could have a look at it.

From a distance, it all looked the same as the first time she'd seen it. The same imposing and beautiful structure which had so impressed her—straddling the edges of the stark northern moorland she'd grown to love. But as the car drew closer she could see that the façade was nothing but an illusion. She told the driver to stop and she got out, her heart as heavy as a stone. Much of the building had crumbled and was lost—and at the back were just blackened remains where once a home had stood. A grim ghost of a place with paneless windows and no roof or chimney. Jack's beloved Blackwood was nothing but a fragile shell with all the life blown away from it.

Hearing something was not the same as seeing it for yourself and the reality of the destruction made her feel sick. Tears threatened to burn her horrified eyes—but there was no time for tears and she climbed back into the taxi, taking one last forlorn look out of the window. The lawns were wild now and the shrubs badly in need of pruning and with every second that mounted Ashley could feel the painful acceleration of her heart as the car took her towards the Ivy House.

What would she find there? Would blindness and disfigurement have changed Jack beyond recognition?

A woman she didn't know opened the door, and she looked at Ashley with a question in her eyes.

'Can I help you?'

'I'm…a friend of Jack's. I heard about his accident and I've come to see him.'

'I'm sorry, but I'm afraid Mr Marchant isn't seeing any visitors.'

'Please. I think he'll want to see me.' But as she said the words she realised their bitter irony. If Jack was blind then he wouldn't be 'seeing' anyone.

There was a pause while the woman studied her and maybe something in Ashley's plea touched her because she opened the door wider and stepped aside.

'You look harmless enough—and it might do him good to talk to someone for a change. But not for long, mind,' she warned. 'Come this way.'

The woman led the way along a long corridor to a door right at the far end, and she opened it to let Ashley step through and then shut it behind her.

The room was gloomy, the light from the fire its only illumination, and Ashley was trembling as her eyes took in the scene in front of her. Because there, sitting in front of the fire—his head bowed in a way she had never seen it bowed before—sat the blinded form of her lover. His tall frame was still striking but all the energy and vitality seemed to have been sucked from him—as if, just like Blackwood, he were nothing but an empty shell. By his feet sat Casey, who looked up as she entered. The dog's ears pricked and, with a little yelp, he jumped up and ran towards her.

'Down, boy,' said Ashley softly and she saw Jack start.

'Who's that?' he demanded, putting his head to one side—as if to listen more keenly. 'Is that you, Mary?'

'No, it is not Mary. Don't you know who it is?' She swallowed. 'Casey does.'

Blindly, he reached out his hand towards her and the gesture nearly broke Ashley's heart. 'Who *is* it?' he repeated. 'God, am I going mad at last? For a minute then I thought—'

She could not help herself—her hand reached out and entwined with the outstretched fingers of his.

'What did you think?' she whispered.

'But that is her voice,' he said, like a man in a dream as his fingers now locked around hers. 'And this is her hand in mine. Ashley? Ashley? Is that really you?'

'Yes.' She swallowed. 'Yes, it's me, Jack.'

'Not a dream?'

'No dream, no—although maybe it feels a bit like one.'

'Let me touch you. Let me touch you properly.'

She had thought that he meant to kiss or to caress her, but Ashley realised that for Jack touch had taken on a whole new dimension. His fingers had become his eyes. As she bent towards him they reached up to her face—their feather-light contact tracing the contours of her features as if he was learning them all over again.

'So it really is you,' he said wonderingly. 'Ashley Jones.'

'Yes.'

'And you've come back to me?'

'Yes, I've come back to you.'

'Well, you shouldn't have bothered,' came his harsh assertion and Ashley stilled as he let her hand fall—turning his head away and waving her away in a gesture of dismissal. 'You should have stayed where you were and forgotten all about me.'

'What are you talking about?'

'For God's sake, Ashley,' he grated. 'Don't let your tender heart blind you to the truth—or to reality. You've seen me—so now go.'

'And if I don't want to go?'

'You have no choice in the matter. I'm telling you to go. You think I deserve someone like you, after what I did to you?' He shook his head and bit the words out as if they were poison. 'I'm not the man you need—especially now that I have a disability. And maybe that's my punishment for having lied to you and misled you for so long. For having taken your innocence with scant regard for anything except my own pleasure.' His voice deepened with some kind of emotion which made it sound as if it was close to breaking. 'But don't worry, Ashley—nobody will blame you for not wanting me. Not even me. Especially not me. I'm blind—and it's the perfect let-out clause.'

She could feel the walls pressing in on her—and her heart felt as if it were being squeezed by some ruthless and powerful fist. 'And what if I told you that I don't want a "let-out" clause?' she demanded quietly. 'If I said that I didn't care about your blindness? That you are still Jack—my Jack—and you always will be—and that no disability could be greater than the one of not having you in my life any more?'

'Stop it right now! Stop it,' he raged. 'You think I'm in any position to withstand your sweet words of comfort? It's over, Ashley—and I've accepted that. So go. You once told me that you didn't think you could ever trust me again, and that no relationship could ever be founded on a lack of trust, and you were right.'

'But I believe in my heart that you would never abuse my trust again.'

'You're just saying that to placate me,' he said, from between gritted teeth. 'Because I am blind and you pity me.'

'And barring maybe one occasion, since when did I ever say things to you that I didn't mean?'

At this he said nothing. Seconds passed—or maybe they were minutes—and Ashley's breath caught in a throat which was as dry as bushfire although she could feel the wet pricking of tears in her eyes. Until suddenly he reached for her—his hand moving from her shoulders down to her waist and then to the curve of her hip. And something of the old, masterful Jack was back as he gathered her towards him and pulled her down into his lap.

'Do you really mean that?' he demanded.

'I really do. Every single word. Every syllable.'

Her heart was racing as she pushed a lock of raven hair back from his brow—across which now ran a livid scar, an ugly raised ridge of a thing. She looked into the ebony eyes which once had been so brilliant and gleaming but which now looked back at her, opaque and sightless. And her heart turned over with sorrow and regret—but mainly with love. Pure and deepest love that no scar could ever diminish. 'Jack,' she breathed. 'My sweet, darling Jack.'

'Kiss me,' he instructed unsteadily. 'Just kiss me once, Ashley, and convince me that I'm not dreaming this—and that any moment I'll awake to nothing but empty arms and a cold memory.'

She lowered her lips to his and as his mouth brushed over hers she cried out at the poignant sweetness of that first contact. 'Oh, Jack,' she breathed again. 'My darling, darling Jack.'

The kiss went on for countless minutes, and for Ashley it said everything that needed to be said. It healed and it consolidated. It comforted and renewed. She wondered if he felt it too—that utter sense of unity, of two lost souls and hearts who had found each other again.

When the kiss ended, he threaded his fingers in her hair. 'You're wearing it loose,' he observed unevenly.

'Yes. I do that more often these days.' And then, because she was acutely aware of how precious these moments were—that they could determine their whole future—she forced herself to confront reality. 'What happened?' she whispered. 'What happened to you?'

'To blind me? You mean you haven't heard?'

She shook her head—until she realised that such gestures would no longer do. 'No,' she said instead. 'I knew you'd been injured, but that's all. And as soon as I heard that—I came.'

His fingers played with the spill of her hair, just as they used to do after he'd made love to her. 'Where do I begin? With the obvious, I suppose. After you'd gone, my life seemed… I don't think there's a single word which could define it. Empty. Incomplete. Aching. I'd never experienced such a feeling before—not even when I'd been in active service. It was as if I'd lost a part of myself. And the worst part of all was knowing that it had been my own fault—that if I'd been truthful with you from the start, then you might still be with me.' He gave a ragged sigh. 'Until I told myself that you were so pure and fundamentally innocent that you would never have begun an affair with me if you'd known I was married.'

Again, she smoothed a thick lock of raven hair away from his eyes, thinking that it was longer than he usually liked to wear it. And then she kissed his scarred brow for good measure and saw his lips curve briefly in response.

'Did you know that my wife has died?' he questioned suddenly.

In his arms, Ashley stiffened. 'No.'

'So you came back in spite of that?' he mused.

To be honest, she hadn't even stopped to consider it—her thoughts had all been about his welfare, not their future. And yet when she'd seen him, she had gone straight into his arms like a homing pigeon—as if Jack *was* her future. But wasn't that leaping ahead of herself?

'What happened to her?' she whispered.

'The very same morning you left—I had a phone call from the clinic to say that she'd passed away peacefully during the night.'

She remembered the phone ringing as she had slipped silently from the house and her own determination to close the door on her life at Blackwood.

'I thought of contacting you to tell you—but realised it would make no difference. I knew that I had no right to see you—and I resigned myself to the fact that you were gone from my life for ever. But my heart felt shattered and my sleeping became worse again—although, ironically, the biography I was writing was working well. It became a kind of refuge for me—as work so often can be. I took to going to bed later and later in order to put off the inevitable moment of lying in a bed which seemed so empty—and wishing that you were still there in my arms.

'One night while I was reading, I fell asleep in the chair—and a spark from the fire hit the rug. I must have been more exhausted than I'd realised because I slept through the initial smoulder—and by the time I awoke, the fire had taken hold.'

'Oh, Jack.'

'That extinguisher we kept in the hall didn't even make a dent in it. I called the fire brigade and then I ran to one of the outhouses and found a hose. I was standing spraying water at the front façade of the house when a beam came toppling down and hit me in the face.' There was a pause. 'And when I awoke, I found myself in hospital with my eyes bandaged and Blackwood no more.'

'And can you see anything?'

He stared straight ahead and screwed up his dull eyes. 'I can just about make out the glow of the fire. And the vague outline of that piano over there.'

'And anything else? Can you see me?'

'No, my angel—but holding you and hearing you is enough.'

She thought how thin he looked, and how pale—and her fingers crept up to the recalcitrant lock of hair. 'Your hair needs combing,' she observed.

'Am I so repulsive to you, then, Ashley?'

She pretended to consider it, just as she would have done before. 'You know you can't start blaming your blindness for *everything*, Jack!'

At this, he laughed and then shook his head in wonder. 'Witch!' he murmured as he bent his head to her ear. 'You know, I never thought I'd laugh or smile again—and yet just ten minutes in your company and I'm doing both.'

'Ah, but I can't promise that will be representative of our life together. I may soon drive you mad.'

There was a pause. 'I'm pretending I didn't hear that.'

'Well, I'd rather you didn't, otherwise I could accuse you of ignoring me—which would be a bit much since I've travelled all this way to see you.'

'You mean you want a life together?'

'Of course I want a life together—I want to be with you for the rest of my life. I can't bear the thought of anything else. Why else do you think I'm sitting on your lap and kissing you whenever I get the opportunity?' She placed her lips over his and just breathed him in.

'Now I know why they say love is blind,' he said mockingly.

Ashley bit back a smile. How irreverent he was! And she realised then that nothing could ever lessen the vibrant life-force which was Jack Marchant. She bent to kiss the tip of his nose and to feel the warmth of his skin against hers. 'I'm going to make us both some tea—and after that we're going for a walk. I'm going to describe all the spring flowers to you and tell you about the way the sun is shining on the grass and then we can stop, and listen to the birdsong. When did you last go outside, Jack?'

He shook his head. 'I don't remember. And as pressing and as entertaining as both those proposals are—there's something which will always take priority, Ashley.'

It was one of those questions which didn't really need asking—but Ashley couldn't resist.

'And what's that?'

He smiled again, his fingertip tracing the upward curve of her lips. 'I'd quite forgotten how well you had learned to flirt. Come closer, my sweet minx—and I'll show you.'

She realised that his sightless eyes could still weep, for she felt the wetness which mingled on their cheeks. But as he bent his head and began to kiss her, Ashley's eyes fluttered to a close to block out everything but the sensation.

And in that moment she was as blind as he was.

EPILOGUE

SHE married him on a soft summer's day in the little village church, near Blackwood. Their only witnesses were Christine and Julia—one a widow and the other a spinster. Two middle-aged women whose own dreams of love had been cut short or never realised—but who looked with deep affection on the couple who made their vows so tremulously in that small church. Ashley wore a simple gown of white cotton and carried a bunch of cream roses she had picked herself from one of the now-wild bushes at Blackwood.

Dismissing the two carers with a generous pay-off, they made their home in Ivy House while Blackwood was being rebuilt—because Jack had discovered he couldn't bear to see the house which had been home to generations of his family simply crumble into the earth. Ashley was charged with overseeing much of the reconstruction—and she determined to use as many local craftspeople as possible to recreate the magnificent manor house which she had grown to love. There would be gleaming floors and sweeping staircases and stained glass just as before—but there would be modern touches, too. More en-suite bathrooms, for a start—and the opportunity to make the huge building more energy-efficient.

To Ashley's delight, Jack continued to write the biography he'd been working on before the fire—he dictated it into a machine and she typed it up for him once she'd completed his novel. But the novel was never published—nor even read by anyone else, much to the chagrin and persistent pleas of Jack's agent. Ashley was no expert, but even she suspected that the explosive and powerful content of the book was enough to ensure a massive global success—and a film was just crying out to be made. She said as much to her husband one evening, when she was lying on the sofa with her head in his lap where she'd just been reading aloud to him.

'I know,' he murmured as he kissed the top of her head. 'But I don't want that kind of success, Ashley. It disrupts. It takes over—devouring what it creates. I have the estates and the farms to provide us with income. In fact, I have everything I want here—with you. Why should I go seeking more?'

She knew exactly what he meant—she'd read enough celebrity magazines to see how fame could corrupt. She could just imagine the field day the publicists would have: *Blind hero writes powerful anti-war polemic!* Their lives would be dissected. He would be like a butterfly pinned to a piece of cardboard—trapped and watched over—this fiercely proud husband of hers.

For a man as independent as Jack, she had thought

that occasionally he would rail and protest against his blindness—but he did not. He seemed content to rely on Ashley for support and guidance—maybe because that support and guidance was reciprocal. For Ashley felt she took from him as much as she gave. She was his eyes, yet he was her heart—and never had the marriage vows seemed to be more applicable than in their case. *One flesh and one blood.*

Until one bright clear morning he startled her by asking whether she was wearing a pale-blue dress.

Ashley spun round and stared at him. 'Why...yes.'

'And some sort of gold necklace?'

It was the one with the beautiful pearls he had ordered for their wedding day. 'Yes!'

Trying not to dare to hope, she made an appointment for them at a top London eye hospital—where, under the care of a brilliant ophthalmologist, Jack's eyesight began to improve until he gradually recovered the sight in one eye. He would never be able to take up flying—or to read the small print of a book without adequate lighting—but he could see enough to gaze at their first son and to see that he had inherited his father's brilliant black eyes.

Ashley was pregnant with their second child when the work at Blackwood was finally completed and the house restored to a glorious and welcoming state. But they never moved into it—because Jack had felt uneasy about the project. Lazy pillow talk had allowed them to discuss the subject at length and he told her that he wanted to turn the house into a respite home for the blind, and for those who cared for them. That he wanted to create a garden for the senses—composed of fragrant herbs and flowers with scented bowers in which to sit and listen to birdsong. The Ivy House was plenty big enough for their growing family and they could always build on if they needed extra space. He wanted Blackwood to become a haven—a warm and welcoming place which could provide comfort and hope for those who needed it.

A family from London's East End had left that very morning and the little six-year-old girl whose mother had been blind since birth had left behind a small pot of lily-of-the-valley she'd picked as a thank-you gift. Ashley buried her nose in the fragrant little bell-shaped flowers and felt a great wave of gratitude for all that they had.

It was quiet and peaceful in the vast hallway now that everyone had gone. She remembered the first time she had seen that hall and how intimidating it had seemed. And she remembered the first time that Jack had led her upstairs to his bed—and how darkly powerful and compelling he had seemed. He still was—her endlessly fascinating partner—her tender and imaginative lover.

They had experienced many trials and tribulations during their time together—but hadn't those trials tested them and made them stronger? Hadn't they helped forge a bond between them which only death could break?

She glanced up to see him walking into the hall to join her, a soft smile curving the edges of his lips as he looked at her and Ashley gave an instinctive little shiver.

All these years down the line and her life with him still felt like a honeymoon.

His voice broke into her thoughts. 'And what are you smiling about so enigmatically, Ashley Marchant?' he questioned.

She touched her fingers to his raven hair, then trailed them down to the edges of those sensual lips. 'Oh, I was just agreeing with whoever it was who wrote "love conquers all".'

'Virgil,' he remarked as he pulled her into his arms and pushed the hair back from her face just before he began to kiss her—his beloved wife. 'It was Virgil.'

He felt the clench of his heart and a deep sense of gratitude for he knew that he was the most fortunate of men. Jack had fought and won many battles in his life— but his marriage to Ashley was his greatest victory of all.

Harlequin *Presents*

Coming Next Month

from **Harlequin Presents® EXTRA.** Available June 14, 2011.

#153 THE MAN WHO COULD NEVER LOVE
Kate Hewitt
Royal Secrets

#154 BEHIND THE PALACE WALLS
Lynn Raye Harris
Royal Secrets

#155 WITH THIS FLING...
Kelly Hunter
P.S. I'm Pregnant!

#156 DO NOT DISTURB
Anna Cleary
P.S. I'm Pregnant!

Coming Next Month

from **Harlequin Presents®.** Available June 28, 2011.

#2999 A STORMY SPANISH SUMMER
Penny Jordan

#3000 A NIGHT OF SCANDAL
Sarah Morgan
The Notorious Wolfes

#3001 AFTER THEIR VOWS
Michelle Reid

#3002 THE WEDDING CHARADE
Melanie Milburne
The Sabbatini Brothers

#3003 ALESSANDRO'S PRIZE
Helen Bianchin

#3004 THE ULTIMATE RISK
Chantelle Shaw

Visit www.HarlequinInsideRomance.com
for more information on upcoming titles!

HPCNM0611

REQUEST YOUR
FREE BOOKS!

Harlequin *Presents*

PASSION GUARANTEED SEDUCTION

2 FREE NOVELS PLUS
2 FREE GIFTS!

YES! Please send me 2 FREE Harlequin Presents® novels and my 2 FREE gifts (gifts are worth about $10). After receiving them, if I don't wish to receive any more books, I can return the shipping statement marked "cancel." If I don't cancel, I will receive 6 brand-new novels every month and be billed just $4.05 per book in the U.S. or $4.74 per book in Canada. That's a saving of at least 15% off the cover price! It's quite a bargain! Shipping and handling is just 50¢ per book in the U.S. and 75¢ per book in Canada.* I understand that accepting the 2 free books and gifts places me under no obligation to buy anything. I can always return a shipment and cancel at any time. Even if I never buy another book, the two free books and gifts are mine to keep forever.

106/306 HDN FC55

Name _____ (PLEASE PRINT)

Address _____ Apt. #

City _____ State/Prov. _____ Zip/Postal Code

Signature (if under 18, a parent or guardian must sign)

Mail to the **Reader Service:**
IN U.S.A.: P.O. Box 1867, Buffalo, NY 14240-1867
IN CANADA: P.O. Box 609, Fort Erie, Ontario L2A 5X3

Not valid for current subscribers to Harlequin Presents books.

**Are you a current subscriber to Harlequin Presents books
and want to receive the larger-print edition?
Call 1-800-873-8635 or visit www.ReaderService.com.**

* Terms and prices subject to change without notice. Prices do not include applicable taxes. Sales tax applicable in N.Y. Canadian residents will be charged applicable taxes. Offer not valid in Quebec. This offer is limited to one order per household. All orders subject to credit approval. Credit or debit balances in a customer's account(s) may be offset by any other outstanding balance owed by or to the customer. Please allow 4 to 6 weeks for delivery. Offer available while quantities last.

Your Privacy—The Reader Service is committed to protecting your privacy. Our Privacy Policy is available online at www.ReaderService.com or upon request from the Reader Service.

We make a portion of our mailing list available to reputable third parties that offer products we believe may interest you. If you prefer that we not exchange your name with third parties, or if you wish to clarify or modify your communication preferences, please visit us at www.ReaderService.com/consumerschoice or write to us at Reader Service Preference Service, P.O. Box 9062, Buffalo, NY 14269. Include your complete name and address.

HPII

USA TODAY *bestselling author B.J. Daniels*
takes you on a trip to Whitehorse, Montana,
and the Chisholm Cattle Company.

RUSTLED

Available July 2011 from Harlequin Intrigue.

As the dust settled, Dawson got his first good look at the rustler. A pair of big Montana sky-blue eyes glared up at him from a face framed by blond curls.

A woman rustler?

"You have to let me go," she hollered as the roar of the stampeding cattle died off in the distance.

"So you can finish stealing my cattle? I don't think so." Dawson jerked the woman to her feet.

She reached for the gun strapped to her hip hidden under her long barn jacket.

He grabbed the weapon before she could, his eyes narrowing as he assessed her. "How many others are there?" he demanded, grabbing a fistful of her jacket. "I think you'd better start talking before I tear into you."

She tried to fight him off, but he was on to her tricks and pinned her to the ground. He was suddenly aware of the soft curves beneath the jean jacket she wore under her coat.

"You have to listen to me." She ground out the words from between her gritted teeth. "You have to let me go. If you don't they will come back for me and they will kill you. There are too many of them for you to fight off alone. You won't stand a chance and I don't want your blood on my hands."

"I'm touched by your concern for me. Especially after you just tried to pull a gun on me."

"I wasn't going to shoot you."

Dawson hauled her to her feet and walked her the rest of the way to his horse. Reaching into his saddlebag, he pulled out a length of rope.

"You can't tie me up."

He pulled her hands behind her back and began to tie her wrists together.

"If you let me go, I can keep them from coming back," she said. "You have my word." She let out an unladylike curse. "I'm just trying to save your sorry neck."

"And I'm just going after my cattle."

"Don't you mean your boss's cattle?"

"Those cattle are mine."

"*You're* a Chisholm?"

"Dawson Chisholm. And you are…?"

"Everyone calls me Jinx."

He chuckled. "I can see why."

Bronco busting, falling in love…it's all in a day's work.
Look for the rest of their story in

RUSTLED

Available July 2011 from Harlequin Intrigue
wherever books are sold.

THE NOTORIOUS
WOLFES

A powerful dynasty,
where secrets and scandal never sleep!

Eight siblings, blessed with wealth, but denied the one
thing they wanted—a father's love. Haunted by their
past and driven to succeed, the Wolfes scattered to the
far corners of the globe. It's said that even the blackest
of souls can be healed by the purest of love….

But can the dynasty rise again?